T0198659

Blood
Hold

Roxanna Kay

iUniverse, Inc.
New York   Bloomington

Blood Hold

This is a work of fiction. All of the characters, names, incidents, organizations, and dialogue in this novel are either the products of the author's imagination or are used fictitiously.

iUniverse books may be ordered through booksellers or by contacting:

iUniverse
1663 Liberty Drive
Bloomington, IN 47403
www.iuniverse.com
1-800-Authors (1-800-288-4677)

ISBN: 978-1-4401-9843-4 (sc)
ISBN: 978-1-4401-9844-1 (ebk)

Printed in the United States of America

iUniverse rev. date: 12/10/2009

Also by Roxanna Kay

Triple Cap

Rikki Rankin, a ruthless Private Investigator/Bounty Hunter, is accused of killing Vanessa. Public knowledge of threats Rikki made against Vanessa, along with other evidence stacked-up against her, makes her the prime suspect.

The passion Detective Hayes once felt for Rikki has turned into an obsession to ruin her.

Two friends help her steal a boat so she can elude law enforcement. Betrayed by one of them, she braves the waters of Lake Tenkiller alone.

Rikki's assistant, Grace, finds her beaten and unconscious and joins the quest to clear her name.

Amidst it all, Rikki manages to make a love connection.

TRIPLE CAP is an amazing race across Lake Tenkiller with all the elements of betrayal, murder, obsession, love of friends and a blossoming romance with laugh-out-loud humor.

Acknowledgements

M̲Y̲ COUSIN, CRICKET LETOURNEAU, your support has been never-ending. We have shared everything two cousins possibly could—and we are still alive to tell about it! I'm looking forward to our future adventures! You will never know how grateful I am for you...love you!

Stephen Maples your encouragement kept me going many times as I wrote this book. You were there through my weak moments. Saying thanks doesn't seem like enough, for the times you picked me up, told me to stop whining and get to writing. You are a huge part of this book...inside and out. *Wa do!*

Janet Augerhole, I appreciate the hours you spent looking over my manuscripts, giving me your input! And the hours we've spent around a good ol' campfire, laughing until our cheeks and abs (of steel) hurt! Don't get no better than that. Herman Augerhole (Roy), well you're just Herman. Keep your britches up—nobody wants to see your bum! Did I ever thank you for nicknaming me Crazy Cora? I'm pretty sure I didn't...

Ray and Sandy Gipson, being able to go to your house and relax has been invaluable! Thanks for all the good dinners, drinks and campfires! Ray, you're the only one that makes me my favorite meal! Also, the only one brave enough to wrestle me to the wet ground. Thanks guys for all you do.

Tracy Christie, thank you for keeping my computer up and running with your IT expertise. You're the best...not to mention *u-de-le-ga*!

Bill Payne, Cliff & Katie in the morning on 107.1 KTFX, thanks for your support!

Wa-do, Anna Sixkiller you're guidance with the Cherokee Language was invaluable.

Renee Kinkead the time you spent with me shooting the cover and back cover photo is greatly appreciated! Thanks for all your input.

In Remembrance:

Mighty Joe Young – Tahlequah, Oklahoma

May 20, 1963 – October 8, 2008

You kept me laughing! Everyone at Ned's will miss you, Mighty Joe Young!

Stephen Maples this one's for you, Cowboy.
You know why.

rk

1

GRACE WAS IN THE middle of her morning routine when Rikki arrived at the office. The coffee aroma tantalized Rikki's taste buds. She wished she liked the taste as much as the smell. As it were, Grace knocked-back the whole pot, while Rikki guzzled Diet Mountain Dew.

"*O-si-yo* (hello), hoe-down." Rikki ragged on Grace, speaking in Cherokee. She was wearing a red bandana shirt—it reminded Rikki of a hillbilly hoedown with hay bales and fiddles.

Grace held up a finger and continued de-bugging the office with the Super Sweep equipment as she did each morning. Rikki was paranoid with good reason, at least every other month they found a phone tap, a listening device or tracking devices on their vehicles. Grace was fixated on the lights that began to bounce, a bug was discovered. She bent at the waist to look underneath the coffee table, mounted underneath was a wireless audio transmitter.

"I said hellooo..." Rikki sensed dread on Grace's face then she caught the sight of the lights blinking on the Super Sweep. "Aaahhh crap, I spilled my coffee! Grace, *nu-la* (hurry), help me with this!" Rikki yelled as Grace pointed down at the coffee table.

When Rikki spilled her imaginary coffee, it was code for 'time to pow-wow in the equipment room.' High-tech electronic locks kept the equipment room secure. If you weren't Grace or Rikki, you weren't getting in.

"Geeze Louise, I can't believe you just spilled that whole cup of coffee. I'll get a towel." Grace played along.

Rikki entered the codes to unlock the equipment room door, and then did a little jig to the sound of the locks that hummed then clanked as the deadbolt receded.

"I love that sound," Grace responded to Rikki's dance with a whisper.

"Me too...it's so definite and official...we're like real private dicks." Rikki joked about her long career as a private investigator and bounty hunter with Grace at her side as the voice of reason.

The lock made its final adjustment. Rikki raised her arms and shook her hips for the grand finale. Grace couldn't help but giggle as they bolted inside and shut the door. The back wall of the equipment room was lined with shelves stocked with every gadget imaginable.

Rikki's motto was "You're Only As Good As Your Equipment." Across the room a countertop held three desktop computers and two laptops, each with its own specialty. On another wall was an oversized sofa where Rikki had spent more nights than she cared to admit.

As Rikki fumbled around for the light, Grace folded her arms and glared at her. "Gaw, I feel your vibe invading my space even in the dark...No, I haven't called Jaxon back," Rikki whispered as she turned around to face Grace.

Jaxon Drywater lived on Lake Tenkiller and helped Rikki clear her name when Greg Hayes accused her of murder six months earlier. Truth be told, he had Rikki from "hello" but she wouldn't acknowledge or act on it. He was a six-foot tall, Cherokee man with silky black hair and eyes to match. It was his integrity Rikki found appealing. His strong, sexy jaw-line didn't hinder matters either—everything Rikki ever wanted in a man. They had a connection from the moment they met but until six months ago they hadn't realized the passion they shared. Now Rikki shut him out and wouldn't even return his calls, which infuriated Grace.

"It's been six months, call him already. I'm so sick of being in the middle of this madness, Rikki," Grace whispered back. "Furthermore..."

"Furthermore? You don't say "furthermore". Does that mean you really mean business?" Rikki was amused. "A girl's gotta do whata girl's gotta do to protect herself from the mens."

"Why do you always sabotage your relationships?"

"We kissed, that was it...it never was a relationship. It was just *a-da-ta-we-do-di* (kiss). You know full well I've been married three times and have no intentions of doing *that* again. I don't wanna get close to anyone. However, I did call Jackson last night...for a booty call...guess I forgot to tell you." Rikki whispered with a big grin, exposing pearl white teeth and one dimple on her right cheek.

"What? You called Jaxon Drywater for a booty call and didn't tell me. What happened?" Grace was thrilled more for Jaxon than Rikki.

"Well, I called Jackson but it was...Brad Jackson...doesn't that count? Jaxon...Jackson all the same...just men." Rikki cracked herself up!

"You're the frickin' hoe-down. I give up. Let me say one last time...Jaxon cares for you more than you deserve...whatever...I'll stop trying." Grace threw her hands in the air.

"Well thank God you're finished...'cause we have to figure out who bugged the lobby. Did anyone come in this morning? Oh, yeah, I was just kiddin' about the booty call thing...it didn't happen. I actually spent a lovely evening with Gunner and Mallie."

Rikki's son, Gunner, was sixteen and her daughter, Mallie, fifteen. The love Rikki held back from everyone else gushed out onto her kids. They never knew anything other than being raised by a single mom who strapped on a weapon every morning. It was the three of them against the world.

"You're impossible...and nobody's been here this morning. You didn't write down what locks you locked last night...so I couldn't unlock the door. Good job, Sherlock."

Seven deadbolt locks decorated the front door of the office. Four different ones were bolted each night then coded on a dry erase board in Rikki's office. A little over-the-top, yes, but that's Rikki.

"So it had to be yesterday. There's no sign of forced entry. Besides someone would have to be crazy to try and break in here with all our security...think back, who came in yesterday?" Rikki racked her brain to remember.

"Mailman, that one kid that skateboards around here came in and tried to sell me some candy. Those attorneys came in... doubt it was them though."

"I'm rulin' out the mailman...what about this kid? I'll find him later and grill him till he cries." Rikki was fuming on the inside. "Let's just leave the bug in place and talk about off-the-wall crap. Make 'em wish they weren't listenin'."

"This should be fun. Okay, I'm ready...let's go." Grace maneuvered toward the door.

"Let's do it, too it." Rikki trailed behind her.

"Rikki, have you banged the mailman? You ruled him out awful fast. Sad I even have to ask such a question." Grace mumbled.

Giggle. "Ask me when we get to the lobby. Oh, yeah...I should tell ya, I had the dream about my mom last night," Rikki warned.

"Oh great...that's never a good sign of what's to come," Grace said as they walked out of the equipment room. The door automatically locked behind them.

"I think it's a great sign...it means I've got a challenge ahead of me...I love it." They reached the lobby and changed the conversation right on queue.

"Grace, should I go home and change my clothes? These coffee stains are not attractive." Rikki performed for the eavesdroppers.

"It's up to you...I hardly even notice it though." Grace giggled under her breath. "Hey have you ever banged the mailman?"

Way to dive right in to that conversation, Grace. Rikki released a deep throaty giggle. "Funny you should ask...*no*! But he has nice thighs. Have you ever noticed his massive muscular thighs?"

"Oh gawd...I know! We love good thighs." Grace played along.

"I know...I really wanted to reach out and touch someone the other day when he delivered the mail in his sexy little uniform shorts." Rikki looked at Grace widened her eyes and smiled. Grace put her head in her hands trying not to laugh out loud.

"Oh Mylanta, you ain't right!" Grace lured Rikki away from the conversation. She knew Rikki would elaborate, taking the conversation to a whole new level.

Deep throaty giggle again. "Don't ask if you don't want to know. What the heck?"

"Hey Rikki, have you noticed the cuss bucket has been empty for like a week now? You just said heck instead of hell. I'm proud of you."

"Wow, I didn't even think about it...cool. I have noticed I have a lot more dollars to spend. Hey look what I can do..." Rikki kicked her leg behind her, tilted her head and smiled. Grace's brows folded inward as she compared Rikki's actions to a four year old child.

"You're stupid! I've got cramps...think I'm gonna start my period." Grace tossed in just for grins. She knew it would disgust Rikki.

Rikki snarled her lip and rolled her eyes at Grace. "I wondered why you look so bloated. Are you craving red meat and chocolate?"

"Shut-up! Well...yes, maybe a little."

Wonder if they've heard enough of this crap. Rikki flashed a glimpse at the listening device. "Hey come hither, I wanna show you a new format I came up with to do my reports." Rikki skipped to her office on an energy overload.

"I wondered what you were working on so hard," Grace said as she shadowed Rikki to her office. She had no clue what

Rikki was talking about, but played along anyway. "You need a Ritalin!"

"Evidently you think I got too much oomph in my step?" Rikki sat in front of her computer and began typing with the speed of bionic fingers:

Let's go for a drive. There's got to be a van or something around here receiving all this good information. I don't need a Ritalin...you do!

"Wow that looks really good. I like it a lot." Grace answered in code, actually meaning, she agreed they should look for the culprit.

Grace pushed the activation button on the alarm as they wondered out the back door. Rikki leaned against the nose of her truck then looked around for something out of the ordinary. Both giggled at the stupid conversation their stalker had to hear for their entertainment.

A flicker from a reflection and a thunderous crash made Rikki leap towards Grace. The truck window shattered as she snatched her up and flung her to the ground. Rikki landed on top of a scared-stiff Grace. Grace laid in fetal position in front of the truck. On her belly Rikki crawled swiftly around to the driver's side of the truck, expecting Grace to be behind her.

"Stay down!" Rikki yelled above the ringing in her ears.

She pulled a 9mm from the back of her jeans and hid behind the truck searching desperately for the culprit. The Apache Indian blood in her boiled—this was war.

Grace covered her head, her ears rang, her guts churned and tears filled her eyes. Rikki lay under the truck and searched for the shooter's feet. Through narrow eyes she scanned down to the back of the truck then back up again.

"Nnnnn...nnnnn...ooooo!" Rikki blinked. It all happened so fast.

Grace's red cowboy boots that matched her red bandana shirt were sandwiched between a pair of black work boots.

Sweet Jesus, he's got Grace. Breathe. Think. Tsi-sa (Jesus) *give me strength.*

"Rikki Rankin! If you're such a bad ass...show your face!" Greg Hayes yelled. "Now or Grace gets a bullet in the head!"

Rikki gradually stood to her feet. She looked through the windows to see Greg Hayes holding Grace with one arm and his hand over her mouth. He held a .357 revolver to her head with the other hand. Rikki's wits were on overload—how could she get Grace away from him?

Grace was milky white with fear bulging from her tear-filled eyes.

Rikki coolly walked around to the front of the truck where Hayes held Grace hostage. Her finger caressed the trigger of the 9mm pistol at her side. Backing down wasn't an option.

Dead a-s-ga-ya (man), Rikki's eyes were narrow and black, lips taut and she was focused. *Lord I need a straight shot, just one good shot.* She was aware the only way out was to kill him. He wasn't going to allow them to walk away.

"Rikki drop your gun! You are not in control now. Tell me how it feels! Do you wanna see Grace get a bullet through the head?" Hayes rattled on aimlessly.

He's nervous, can't follow through with a thought. Be careful and confident. Rikki coached herself as she analyzed his erratic actions. Hayes continued to ramble. She turned a deaf ear to him.

Come on Grace, look at me. Trust me. Get it together. Grace's terrified eyes darted in every direction, trying to figure out who had a death grip on her.

Grace finally got trapped in Rikki's stare. She was determined to focus on Rikki. *There you are...come on, Grace, follow my eyes.* Rikki shot her eyes to the ground and straight back up to Grace's eyes. She hoped Grace's attention wasn't lost breaking eye contact like that.

Grace knew Rikki was her lifeline and she wasn't about to break contact. *What Rikki? What do I do? Get me out of this!*

Rikki perceived the questions and terror in her eyes as the tears vanished and she scrutinized Rikki's actions.

Atta girl Grace...watch me. I'm not leavin' here without you... tla a-s-ka-hi-yi (no fear). Rikki scarcely nodded her head to let Grace know it was going to be all right. Once again she shot her black eyes to the ground. She knew Grace was getting it from the look in her eyes. They've had the capability to communicate without words for years. They knew each other that well.

"I said drop your gun or I will pump lead into Grace's head!" Hayes screamed, his anger magnifying at Rikki's calm demeanor. He wanted so badly to see her sweat, to see fear in her eyes before he killed her. Rikki would never give him that satisfaction.

It's time, Grace. We only get one shot at this. Please don't let the fear stop you. Rikki nodded slightly at Grace again.

I'm ready Rikki. Grace blinked hard.

Rikki raised her gun. *Lord, I gotta have perfect timing, guide this bullet.*

"Tell ya what...I'll shoot her myself...if that's what I have to do to kill you. It will be my pleasure, really. Think you can beat me?" Rikki still locked into Grace's eyes as she challenged Hayes. He wouldn't expect that from her. She raised her gun further and aimed it at Grace's head.

"What the...? There's no way you'd pull that trigger...you are a wild Indian!" Hayes was shocked that Rikki pointed her gun at Grace's head.

Grace went limp and pushed her weight against Hayes then dropped to the ground with the weight of the world on her shoulders. Rikki drew in a deep breath and squeezed the trigger as she exhaled. Her eyes were big as she watched the bullet that seemed to be moving in slow motion. *Not yet please don't get there yet...Oh God...don't let it hit her. Get down Grace!*

Hayes, dumbfounded, realized he lost his grip on Grace and Rikki had fired a shot. He pointed his gun at Rikki, his blood was scorching, and he so badly wanted to see her die.

Now! Now! Hit him now! Nu-la (hurry)! The bullet struck Hayes in the heart, where only milliseconds ago Grace's head was resting. Hayes staggered backwards and hovered in the air before bouncing off the concrete to his death. Grace landed on the ground at his feet.

Did that really just happen? Rikki was stunned trying to comprehend what had just transpired. Blood splattered on Grace's head. *Please let Grace be all right. I know I didn't miss. Breathe.* She was scared to take a closer look. A moment of self-doubt had her breaths short and shallow.

Rikki approached Hayes' body and booted his gun out of reach. She reached for Grace; she lay on the cement unresponsive.

"Grace! It's over get up! Get up!" She panicked, but managed to grab her cell phone with shaking hands and dial 911.

"It's Rikki Rankin, I need assistance at 91st and Memorial... my office is behind the strip mall."

"What is your emergency?"

Rikki paused she didn't want to say it out loud. The truth of just killing someone was unsettling. "I shot someone."

"Could you speak up I couldn't hear you."

"I shot someone," Rikki said louder. "I shot Greg Hayes. Please send an ambulance." Rikki shut the cell phone and dropped it to the ground then squatted down beside Grace. For a brief moment Rikki rested her whirling head in her hands, the pit of her stomach was heavy in her throat.

"Grace?" She studied the way Grace laid on the ground at Hayes' feet. "Grace?"

The upper half of her body faced up while the lower half was twisted sideways. *Did she hit her head? Did she pass out?*

Rikki went into First Responder mode. Careful not to move Grace she checked for a pulse. *Oh thank God.* She found a pulse. She checked her breathing faint but there. She rubbed Grace's chest with her knuckles applying substantial pressure, to engage the fight or flight mode, hoping Grace would come too.

Grace jerked. Rikki was searching for any injuries. Blood draped the scene, including Grace, and Rikki couldn't tell if it was Grace's blood or Hayes' blood.

"Rikki, I quit," Grace's voice quivered.

"Just be still...an ambulance is on the way. I want you to get checked out. Grace I'm so sorry. But don't be a sissy and quit on me! We've worked too hard," Rikki didn't accept Grace's resignation.

"You saved my life," Grace whispered.

"Guess so."

"Of course...if it weren't for you I wouldn't have been in this situation either."

"Guess so. Ya know, I knew Hayes would surface again but not like this. I bet he was just released from jail." Rikki agonized over Hayes actions.

"Well, let's see...you humiliated him, got him fired and sent to jail. I'd say you pretty much totally ruined his life, that's what I'm thinkin' anyway. Will you tell me the dream about your mom?"

"You've heard it before."

"Not since we were like sixteen...for some reason it'll bring me comfort right now." Grace wanted to think about anything other than the fact she was nearly shot by either a bad guy or her best friend.

Seated on the pavement beside Grace, Rikki crossed her legs Indian style. Hayes never moved again.

"Alright. I'm a little girl skating in circles at the skating rink." Rikki spoke softly. "I have really long hair that hangs down past my butt and flows behind me as I skate. At the other end of the skating rink I see my mom. She had died two months earlier. I skate my heart out trying to get to her but I can't reach her no matter how hard I try. It feels like the skating rink keeps getting longer and longer. I finally get closer and I can see her smile, her dimples. Her arms are folded. I'm soaking up the sight of her standing in front of me, I'm so happy I'm about to bust. I finally reach her and I open my arms ready to just fall into her arms and hug her. She unfolds her arms like she's going to reach for me... her arms fall off. Shockwaves went all through my body. I wanted to feel her hold me one more time. I start to cry."

"All of a sudden I feel this overpowering peace devour my whole body. I hear her sweet voice say, Rikki, you may not be able to hug me or touch me but know that I am with you always, protecting you." Rikki fell silent. *Wa-do e-u-tsi* (Thanks my mother).

Rikki's mom died in a car wreck when Rikki was in the sixth grade and the dreams began a few months later. Rikki and Grace realized the dream occurred just before one of life's turmoil's struck. Through the years Rikki learned to find strength in the dream—maybe too much.

"Thanks, Rikki," Grace said after a few minutes.

"No thanks needed," Rikki's thoughts drifted from the dream to almost shooting her best friend in the head. The mere thought of it made her sick to her stomach.

Sirens were approaching. Rikki pulled herself up with one hand against the building. Her jaws tingled and guts churned, relief came in the form of Diet Mountain Dew spewing everywhere. She wiped her eyes, spit and shook her head in an effort to shake it off and gain control.

The ambulance pulled into the parking lot along with four Tulsa Police cars. Following shortly behind were Channel Six News and Channel Eight News satellite vans.

Grace tried to push herself up with her elbows.

"Grace, lay down! Please just be still a minute." Rikki stood over her bound and determined not to let her up.

"Bossy!" Grace didn't move though.

"Over here!" Rikki yelled at the ambulance guys. "Oh wow, Grace, they are hot," She whispered down to Grace.

"I wanna see!" Nice distraction from her current predicament.

"Oh you will. They are headin' right toward you."

"How's my hair? Omigod...Rikki...you just killed a man!"

"I know...we don't have to worry about Greg Hayes anymore though...and your hair, well, it's *gi-ga*."

"What? Don't speak Cherokee to me right now. I can't think straight as it is."

"It's bloody...be still. Check out that one's hind-quarter, nice. Do you concur?"

"Let me see it," Grace strained her neck looking at the paramedics. "Yes, I concur."

"We've got to find the recording device that recorded our conversation...I don't want people thinking you're bloated...I had no idea I'd end up killing the guy that planted the bug."

Rikki's head was still spinning as three Tulsa Police Officers approached her.

Officer Stone Russell was the first one to speak. Rikki hadn't spoken to him since Hayes tried to frame her for murder six months earlier.

"Hey Rikki...what the hell happened here?" All three Officers were assessing the scene.

"It's Greg Hayes. He was gonna kill us both." Rikki didn't want to talk about it.

"We know he had it in for you. Can you fill out a report?"

"I don't have it in me today. Can I come down to the station tomorrow?"

"That's fine. Hey, get those reporters outta here!" Stone yelled to the other officers. He knew Rikki well enough to know she needed time to process what had just happened. Talking to reporters was out of the question.

"Rikki, I don't wanna go to the hospital. Will you call Mike?" Grace was in a panic, twisted sideways on the gurney as they wheeled her by Rikki and the officers.

Grace had dated Mike for five years and he was one of the few good guys left. Respectful, hardworking, generous, and he could put up with Grace's queenliness. He had the 'business in the front-party in the back' style haircut (otherwise known as a mullet), it added to his unwavering good-ole-boy character. His nickname was mullet-man.

"Guys, could you excuse me...I need to see about Grace. Stone, thanks, I don't want to talk to reporters right now."

"No problem...just call me tomorrow and let me know what time you'll be at the station. I'm really sorry you have to go through this Rikki. You were just healing up over the last Greg Hayes episode," Stone showed compassion.

"*Wa-do* (thank you)," Rikki beelined to the ambulance. Officer Stone Russell and the other officers secured the crime scene.

The paramedics examined Grace and determined she could be released without being transported to the hospital. Not that she would've gone anyway.

Red and blue lights flashed all around as Rikki helped Grace inside the building and laid her on the couch in Rikki's office. Rikki sat cocked back in her chair, feet propped up on the desk. They hadn't said a word. Rikki watched Grace sprawled out on the couch. Her blonde hair matted with reddish-brown blood as it dried. The mere thought of her best friend almost getting shot was too much to deal with.

"As soon as the police leave I'll try to find the receiver to that bug." Rikki had to change the direction of her thoughts. "I'll tell Stone about that tomorrow when I go to the station. I wanna get that tape first and see what else he had on me."

"That's probably a good idea." Grace seemed exhausted.

"Are you really gonna quit? Leave me after thirteen years of non-stop fun?" Rikki knew the answer but hoped she was wrong.

"I really am." Grace didn't elaborate.

"Do you wanna shower here? You have blood all over you." Rikki stalled Grace from leaving the office. The thought of her walking out the door, never to return, was more than she could deal with at the moment.

"Think I will." Grace didn't feel like talking much.

While Grace showered, Rikki searched the area for Hayes' vehicle. She found a white van with tinted windows parked at the strip mall not far from the office. The front doors were locked. Rikki checked the back door, knowing it would be locked too but still she had to check.

The door opened. *He must've flown out of here when we walked out the back door.* She tried to imagine what he was thinking. The surveillance equipment inside the van was minimal but enough to record the conversations inside her office. Rikki took the recording device and the tape. She gathered four more tapes and continued to snoop. There was a shrine in her honor.

Wow! That's just scary. She thumbed through some photos Hayes had of her. *Ugly, ugly, oh that's a good one.* There were old newspaper clippings from the Tulsa World about Rikki's volunteer work and various cases she had worked through the years.

According to the notes she found, it was easy to determine he hadn't been doing surveillance on her for long. That day was the first entry, but the background investigation he had performed was very impressive.

2

MORNING ARRIVED WAY TOO soon but Rikki forced herself out of bed and into the shower, hung-over from the p.m. pills she had taken.

It's a new day. Maybe I won't have to kill anyone. She prepared herself for the day as soap ran down her back.

First day without Grace, I don't have a clue. Rikki tried to visualize going to the office without Grace there. Honestly, she had no idea how Grace handled things. For thirteen of the fourteen years that she had owned her own investigation agency Grace handled everything administrative, helped her on research, and kept her out of trouble much of the time.

I took her for granted all these years. She mentally beat herself up.

She stood in front of the mirror. "What am I gonna do without Grace?" She was losing her best friend, her business partner. The mascara in her hand flew across the bathroom. *Screw it!* She was more upset over Grace than killing Greg Hayes.

She wrestled with a pair of tight 501 Levi's and buttoned them. She tugged on a T-shirt with her Private Eye logo on the front and managed to pull it down over her head. The holster That cradled her 9mm snapped into place on the left side of her Levi's. Lastly, she pulled her hair halfway through a ponytail holder and high-tailed it to the office.

Rikki felt no remorse about killing Greg Hayes, but something was different within her being. The general consensus of most people that knew her was that she was disconnected from emotions, cold and rigid. The way she felt now—could anything penetrate that slate of ice?

Rikki went out through the side door into the garage. She stood in surprise at the site of it being half empty. A flashback of her truck window shattering reminded her why the garage was empty. The truck was in the shop. The only vehicle in the garage was a 1995 BMW 325i Convertible. An attorney hired Rikki and racked up thousands of dollars in fees and never paid. She took his car and that was that.

Rikki put the top down on the BMW, pushed the electronic garage door opener, and backed a few feet out of the garage. The morning sun warmed her face, sending her to a serene world that smelled of honeysuckles. Or, it could've been the honeysuckle bush next to the house. Still, a warm sensation went all through her body, but it only lasted for a second.

A voice ripped through the core of Rikki's body, replacing the warm feeling with the urge to draw her gun and randomly shoot. "Rikki? Can you tell us what happened yesterday when you killed Greg Hayes?" Seven reporters approached her car yelling questions and shoving cameras in her face.

Breathe. Don't shoot anyone. Remain calm. She painted on a condescending smile, followed with the typical response. "I have no comment at this time." She pushed down on the accelerator not caring if anyone was behind her. *They should have brains enough to get out of the way of a moving vehicle.*

The office was only a mile from the house, Rikki made it in record time. A drive-by the front of the office revealed more reporters at the front door. She parked in the rear and entered through the back door. No morning coffee smells. No Grace debugging the office. The front door was still locked and it stayed that way. Rikki pushed herself to function. She had the urge to slam everything in her path to the floor, just to watch it break. *Angry much?*

Behind her desk she pilfered through notes that needed to be typed into a report for court the next week. *This is what I can do today. Be productive.* Her hands were crawling all over the keyboard as she escaped the reality of her current situation.

Grace entered through the back door. "Good morning. Did you shoot any reporters on your way in?"

Rikki sat straight up eyes bursting with hope. "Good morning! Are you comin' back to work? I wanted to shoot me a reporter or two, yes...the ones at my house anyway."

"Nope, just came to get my stuff. I spent the night at Mike's, but I've heard they were at my house too." Grace sat the empty box she was carrying on the desk.

Rikki tried to hide the disappointment and downright dread of losing Grace. "I've got to bang out some reports so I'll be right here if ya need me." *O-s-da gi-na-li* (best friend).

"I'll holler at ya when I'm done." Grace lugged a picture of her and her kids off the wall.

Rikki couldn't watch it broke her heart. She settled back down in front of her computer and began to bang on the keyboard again.

Grace buzzed in on the intercom, "Rikki, Channel 6 is on the phone."

"Let's give them the standard, "no comment" answer...don't you think?"

"I don't work here anymore...the call is on line one." Grace pushed the button to disconnect the intercom.

Rikki picked up the phone. "No comment." She hung up the phone.

Grace leaned against Rikki's office door with her arms folded. "That's not how you need to handle those calls."

"Shut-up, you don't work here anymore so don't tell me how to handle my business."

"Hateful." Grace walked out and finished packing, not fazed by Rikki's attitude. She knew Rikki was going through an incredible amount of turmoil having killed a man the day before.

Maybe I should just suck it up. Maybe I shouldn't run out on my best friend after something so traumatic. I gotta take care of me though. Grace was in her own turmoil about leaving Rikki.

Ten minutes later, Grace buzzed Rikki on the intercom again. "Hey, there's someone here to see you."

"Grace, I'm bangin' right now, just have 'em call and make an appointment!" Rikki yelled at the phone.

"Ummm, Rikki you're on speaker phone." Grace looked at the visitor. "It's not what it sounds like."

Rikki's door opened and Jaxon Drywater stood in front of her. She didn't know what to say, she unknowingly ogled him. The last thing Rikki wanted to feel right now was warm and fuzzy inside. Emotions zipped through her uncontrollably, when she thought of their sizzling moment six months earlier. She wanted to run to him and fall apart in his arms. Not going to happen. She fought the urge and it made her angry that she had to.

"Hello, Rikki." His dark eyes were warm and inviting. The way he said her name made her melt like the wicked witch of the west. She wanted to faint. Her heart slammed around in her chest and blocked her air supply. *Gain some composure. Omigod, Jaxon. Wow he looks so good. What do I do? Think of something to say. Why does my brain vapor lock when he's around?*

"I heard what happened, I had to come check on you and Grace. Hope you don't mind."

I do mind...no don't say that out loud. "Have a seat." Rikki showed nothing that was going on inside her.

Dang he's so good-looking. Danger Will Robinson! Ni-hi hi-s-ga-ya u-tso-a-se-di (you man trouble). Rikki knew if she got close to Jaxon someone's heart would break, she didn't want it to be hers. She had spent way too much time protecting herself in that territory.

Grace watched through Rikki's office window. *Don't run Rikki. Stick it out.* Grace so badly wanted Rikki to find love and she knew Rikki could love Jaxon in her own special way.

Awkward silence filled Rikki's office. Rikki stared at Jaxon soaking up the vision of the man that had earned her respect.

He sat before her poised and confident. Their eyes met and Rikki lost all concept of time. The world stop turning and nothing else mattered at that very moment. She gained control over the butterflies in her stomach. Now, if she could just gain control over her rattled heart and her shaky hands.

"*Wa-do* (thank you) for coming by and checking on us," Rikki tried to keep it impersonal.

"*Tsi-lu-gi* (welcome). I couldn't stay away. Did you get any of my messages?" He had to ask.

"I did. Sorry I didn't return your calls but…" she didn't want to explain herself. "Actually, I have no excuse. I just didn't call you back." Frigid and to the point.

"Uh-huh. Rikki, I thought we had a connection and I really want to get to know you on a more personal level."

"Now is not a good time to have this conversation." Rikki was flustered, but held tight to the cold-hearted attitude. She would rather roll in cow manure than talk about her feelings.

"Okay, well sorry I bothered you. I'll leave," Jaxon felt uncomfortable. He stood up to leave. Rikki followed him out to at least give him a proper send off.

Grace was horrified. *Gaw Rikki, why are you so stubborn? You need him. Please don't let him walk out that door.*

Jaxon meandered toward the door as Rikki followed. He suddenly turned and pulled Rikki into his body. Rikki sucked in too much air then melted in his arms.

"I wasn't ready for that." Face to face with Jaxon a nervous giggle escaped her.

"I just had to see if it felt the same as it did six months ago… it does." Jaxon leaned in closer and kissed her. Instantly, Rikki returned to the peaceful world that smelled of honeysuckles. Eyes closed, she let herself enjoy the feel of his touch, the warmth of his breath, his smell.

Way to go Jaxon. Grace cheered him on. *Roll with it Rikki, please don't do anything stupid. Maybe I shouldn't be watching this.* Grace felt like an intruder. She spun in a circle then continued to watch.

Rikki's mind was spinning a mile a minute as Jaxon kissed her. *I can't do this.* She pushed him away.

"I'm *u-yo-a-ye-lv-di* (sorry) this just isn't gonna work for me." She returned to her desk with a sense of relief and a vision in her head of Rocky Payne. *Where did he come from outta nowhere?* Her love life sucked.

Jaxon stood in the doorway of her office and frowned at her disheartened. There was nothing he could say. He disappeared through the door and didn't look back.

Grace sat down on the couch in Rikki's office, crossed her arms and shook her head. She knew there was no need to say anything. She was so fed up with Rikki's attitude. Hopefully it would pass in time. Grace wanted to believe it had something to do with killing Hayes, but she knew better.

The last of her personal items were packed and ready to go. Grace looked around the office. *What am I gonna do without this place, without Rikki?* She didn't want to leave.

They sat in silence.

A split second has changed my whole life. I now have killed a man...actually it may help my business...can't believe I just thought such a thing. I don't know what to do next. What does one do the day after killing another human being? Well, Hayes was borderline human. Rikki was lost in her own morbid thoughts.

Rikki jerked when the phone rang. "Whoa, that scared me," she picked up the receiver, "hello?"

Grace smirked. *That's not how you answer the business phone.*

Rikki glanced at Grace and shrugged her shoulders. She knew what Grace was thinking.

"May I speak to Rikki Rankin?" The caller asked politely.

"She's not in. Can I take a message?"

"Yeah, tell her Teryn Tennin called with channel eight. She has my number."

"I'll tell her." Rikki hung up the phone. "I should talk to her. I like Teryn. She's always done me right. Most of those reporters screw up the facts."

"Yes, you should. Don't hide in your cave right now. Get out there and tell your side of the story. It will probably help your business."

"Get out of my head! I was just thinking that. Grace? Think about just taking some time off. Don't just quit without giving it a lot of thought."

"Get out of my head! I was just thinking that."

Hearing that was huge for Rikki, life didn't seem so bleak.

The back door flew open. "Rikki?"

Grace and Rikki looked at each other with a puckered brow. Rikki got up to see what the commotion was all about.

"There you are. Are you alright?" Cricket grabbed Rikki and hugged her.

"I'm fine." Rikki hugged her cousin and reassured her.

"I've been so worried. How's Grace?"

"I'm fine too, Cricket."

"You two are gonna be the death of me. I've been worried sick." Cricket spent years worrying about Rikki.

"Everything will be fine, stop worrying." Rikki made light of the situation.

The back door opened again and a gang of people poured into the lobby.

"What the...?" Rikki was shaken. "Grace did you know about this?"

"Well...maybe. Guess I should've warned you, so you would've at least brushed your teeth."

Rikki's eyes grew large. "Oh man...I forgot I threw my mascara across the bathroom and walked out. This is not pretty! Jaxon must think I'm a slob! I don't even care. And for the record I did shower and brush my teeth."

"Well, you should've answered your phone last night. Everybody and their dog called me, so I told them to be here at ten. We could use the support."

"I wanted to crawl in my cave and deal with it on my own, Grace."

"I know." Grace smiled and began welcoming everybody.

Rikki and Grace's families were there, as were their friends, clients, and colleagues. Officer Luke Hixon with his wife Mandy, Officer Craig and several other police officers dropped in to support Rikki and Grace.

Deep down Rikki was touched.

Rikki's Dad was the first to approach her. A Cherokee Indian man that never says much, but when he did everyone listened. He hugged his daughter then looked deep in her eyes. Oddly, Rikki saw her pain in his eyes. He pressed his lips together in the form of a slight smile then nodded his head. Rikki knew he was proud of her. Rikki pressed her lips together in the same form and nodded back. He knew, in time, his daughter would be all right. That gesture alone made every emotion Rikki didn't want to feel catch in her throat. She swallowed hard trying to fight back the tears. Choked by the emotions she had been holding back, she disappeared to the restroom.

She filled her hands with cold water and splashed her face. "Wait till you're alone to fall apart." She told herself in the mirror. "Did I brush my teeth?" She parted her lips and looked at her teeth. "I did." A few deep breaths and she had her fearless demeanor back.

Loud knocks on the bathroom door startled her. "Rikki! What are you doin'?" It was her sister, Robin. "Are ya poopin'? Open the door!"

The two were a lot alike in some ways—loud, boisterous, and, at times, downright vulgar. But night and day in other ways, Robin married right out of high school, leading a more normal life. She wore her hair short, framing her face and, if you didn't know her, you would think she was always giving you a dirty look.

The bathroom door opened and Rikki's sister bombarded her with hugs. "You look like crap."

"I'm glad you knew there was a party and got all fixed up. What is up with this anyway? Is this what people do when you shoot someone? Oh, I killed a man, let's have a party!" Rikki was back to her sarcastic self.

"Who cares? There's lots of good food out there. Come on." Robin pushed her sister out into the crowd.

Well-wishers flooded Rikki's office. Grace was being a gracious host as everyone expressed their concern for what had happened to her. Rikki watched for a moment as pride for her best friend consumed her. Grace had handled everything so well.

Rikki crawled up on the desk in the lobby. "May I have your attention, please?" The crowd hushed and inquisitively studied Rikki. "Grace will you join me?"

"You would not be standing on that desk if you knew how much it cost." Grace giggled as she made her way on top of the desk.

"Oh, I'm sure!" Rikki laughed. "I just wanted to thank everyone for coming today. I'm deeply touched by your support. I also wanted to say how proud I am of Grace." Rikki turned to Grace and smiled.

"Thank you." Grace tilted her head slightly as she looked at Rikki. "I would like to thank you for your quick thinking and good aim. Our families could be planning our funerals right now." Grace really put things in perspective for Rikki.

"Ya know...that never even occurred to me. Trust me, I was praying like a son-of-a-gun when I pulled that trigger."

"I don't know how many of you know this, but we do that a lot!" Grace chimed in. "Ya know how you get so scared all you can do is pray? That's about every day around here." Everyone laughed at Grace's honesty.

"Most of you know that Hayes tried to frame me for murder about six months ago and with a little help from my friends I was able to prove it. His plan to ruin me backfired, although he did manage to leave me with a couple of scars. He ended up losing his job as a detective in Cherokee County. Pretty much his life was ruined. Yesterday he went for revenge." Rikki recapped her history with Hayes.

"I know everyone wants to know what happened so I figured I'd just tell you all at once." Rikki saw her Dad sitting in a leather chair in the lobby. He was watching everyone, sizing them up. *So that's where I get it.*

"Grace was debugging the office as she normally does."

"That's not normal!" Robin yelled. Everyone laughed.

"Well, it is for us!" Grace answered.

"Anyway, we found a listening device stuck under that coffee table." Rikki pointed to the table. "After a few minutes of rambling about stupid stuff...that I won't mention...we went out back to look for the receiving end. We weren't outside for a minute when a shot was fired at us." Rikki paused. "I jumped on Grace and we both hit the ground pretty hard."

"I have a black bruise the size of Texas on my hip and leg. Of course, Rikki landed on top of me so she's fine." Grace added.

"Did you want to show us your battle wound?" Rikki teased.

"Sure," Grace tugged at her jeans. "No, Rikki I don't want to show my battle wound!"

"I was just checkin'. Anyway, I moved around to the side of the truck, expecting Grace to be behind me."

"Are you kidding me? I was frozen with fear, I couldn't move! My ears were ringing; it was just an awful feeling. I think I was lying in the fetal position when he pulled me up by the hair."

"I looked under the truck and got the shock of my life. Grace's red boots *and* a pair of work boots! I knew we were in trouble then. I had to do something when Hayes started rambling about putting a bullet through Grace's head. He had his gun against her head. After a few minutes of intense eye communication, Grace dropped to the ground and I pulled the trigger. The bullet hit Hayes in the heart barely missing Grace's head...he died instantly." The image of Greg Hayes falling to the ground replayed in Rikki's head, as she stared off into space.

Stillness filled the room with all eyes on Rikki and Grace, standing atop the desk.

Can she continue? I need to do something! Grace saw a look in Rikki that she had never seen before. *Don't break down now in front of all these people.* Grace couldn't think of anything to say to break the eerie silence. *Stop staring at her!* She wanted to scream at everyone in the room.

Rikki blinked hard, raised her head high, "I've been asked the same question at least a hundred times during my career. Do you really think you could kill a man? The answer has always been "yes." I believe I've proved that now." Rikki slightly smiled. "What I'm battling right now is not feeling remorse. Shouldn't I feel remorse? I'm remorseful for not feeling remorse, does that count?" She made eye contact with several people in the room, wanting someone to answer.

"Maybe you should see about counseling." Someone said from a distance.

Mystified, Rikki and Grace followed the sound of the voice to Rikki's office. Perched on Rikki's desk was Teryn Tennin, cameraman in tow, with cameras rolling.

"Teryn, I didn't know you were invited to my I-killed-a-man party." Rikki remained composed.

"I stopped by to see how you are doing and schedule an interview. You are the breaking story of the week." Teryn smiled, exposing perfect teeth with her long strawberry blonde hair draped around the shoulders of her business suit.

"Uuuhuh. That's real nice. I'm going to say this one time calmly. Turn off your cameras and get out of my office immediately. If I see any of this on the news I will hunt you down and they will never...I do mean never, find the body. Do you understand?" Rikki pressed her lips together with an antagonizing smile. Her eyes were piercing and black.

All eyes shifted to Teryn. She sat still, not even breathing, blue eyes enormous, scared stiff. The cameraman had the same freaked-out gaze as he slowly lowered the camera.

"Oh good grief! Just get up off your skinny, unwelcome butt and get out!" Robin shoved Teryn on the shoulder, disrupting her perfect posture, knocking her off the desk onto her feet.

Without commotion, Rikki's son Gunner, her Dad, her brother, Robert, her nephew, Robby, and brother-in-law, Bruce, had positioned themselves around Teryn and the cameraman.

Her dad undauntedly took the camera and handed it to Gunner. Gunner removed the tape, no words were spoken, and Gunner shoved the camera into the cameraman's chest.

Mallie stood next to her Mema Rita, Rikki's step-mom and her cousin Brooke. They prayed that their family didn't beat the reporter and cameraman to near death. Rita put her arms around Mallie. "Get out of here already. You've done riled the tribe!" Rita yelled out of pity. "The Natives are getting restless!" Rita wasn't Cherokee or Apache but after sixteen years, she understood her family's ways. You mess with one and you've messed with the entire clan.

Teryn made her way through the crowd, stopping at the desk that Rikki and Grace still stood on. "Rikki, I'm really sorry."

"You're sorry because your plan to get the breaking story of the week didn't work, Teryn." Rikki knew the reason behind the apology.

"I didn't mean to be disrespectful. I would still like an interview, if you're willing." Teryn departed with her cameraman.

"All in a day's work!" Grace broke the tension, everyone laughed.

"I really do appreciate all the support. Grace and I are going to be just fine. Grace is going to take some time off effective immediately and I plan to wrap-up the cases I have and take some me time too." Rikki concluded.

Grace added, "I'd like to say 'thanks' to you, Rikki. My life flashed before me, but I knew once I saw the look in your eyes that somehow everything was going to be all right."

Grace hugged Rikki on top of the desk and they made their way down to floor level.

"Let's eat!" Robin started the party again.

Police Officer Stone Russell, pushed his way through the crowd to Rikki. Her eyes lit up when she saw him.

"Oh crap, Stone, I totally forgot about doing that report today."

"I figured you did. You've got your hands full here." He was polite.

"Follow me. We can do it right now in my equipment room."

"I was hoping you would cooperate. I should've had this yesterday...Captain's waiting for my report."

"I know and I appreciate you waiting. I want to get out of this crowd anyway." Rikki punched in the codes for the electronic lock. The deadbolts hummed then clanked as they receded again. Stone smirked at Rikki and shook his head. She grinned and raised her eyebrows. *He likes my locks.*

"Your equipment's better than the department's!" Stone scanned the shelves.

Rikki pulled an office chair away from the counter that held the computers. "Let me get started." She said with dread, as she clicked her pen and began writing the events of the previous day.

3

RIKKI ROLLED AROUND IN her bed irritated. She looked at the clock, 7:11 AM. She discovered the irritating culprit next to the alarm clock. The cell phone buzzed and danced on the nightstand. *What the...? I should've been up an hour ago.*

"Hello?" She answered the phone against her better judgment.

"Rikki? It's Teryn Tennin. I wanted to apologize again for yesterday, I feel really bad about invading your office...crashing your party so to speak. We've always worked well together and I hope I didn't ruin that." Teryn spilled without a breath.

"Teryn...Teryn." Rikki interrupted. "Stop babbling and breathe."

"Sorry, did I wake you?"

"Yes you did, but I should've been up an hour ago so it's okay. I'll tell you what...I'll give you an interview."

"Oh that's great!" Teryn was excited.

"Hang on, hear me out. I want a live on air broadcast. I don't want any editing to this piece. Raw, hard facts and no sugar coating. Can you do it?"

"I'll do it, no matter what it takes." Teryn was already making plans. *How am I going to pull this off?*

"Meet me at my office at ten o'clock. I need to run some errands first."

"I'll be there. Thanks Rikki."

"You bet," Rikki hung up the phone, rolled around in bed a few more minutes, and then made herself get up.

After a shower, hair and make-up, she carefully chose which pair of Levi's to wear with the perfect pair of cowboy boots. She chose black Levi's, black boots, off-white dressy tank top and a black leather jacket. Black holster with her favorite nickel-plated Smith and Wesson 9mm tucked neatly out of sight. *Man, my hair is getting long.* She looked in the mirror at the back of her almost black hair that hung to her lower back. *I need a trim.*

A perfect October day, the air was crisp and sun filled the sky. Rikki drove the BMW with the top up so her hair didn't get tied in knots before the interview. Her sister, Robin, was meeting her at the office at eight-thirty to help out with the phones. She pulled around to the back of the office building, saw the bloodstained asphalt, scanned the area and sat in her car. Flashbacks of shooting Greg Hayes filled her head, the fear in Grace's eyes, the bullet floating through the air. She shook her head to stop the flashbacks. *I gotta stop this. This will not haunt me. Lord, don't let this haunt me.*

Robin pulled up in her PT Cruiser and jumped out smiling. She hurried around her car to Rikki's and abruptly stopped. Rikki knew what she was doing and jumped out of her car.

"Come on, let's get inside." Rikki pulled her arm steering her away from the bloodstain.

"That's a lot of blood. I've never seen anything like that." She tried not to look but her head kept turning toward the bloodstain while Rikki dragged her by the arm.

"I'm gonna have it cleaned, don't want to look at it anymore." Rikki was fighting her own emotions.

Through the back door and down the hall the sound of the phone ringing filled the office. *No coffee smell.* Rikki noted just to torture herself a little more this morning.

"Are you gonna answer that?" Rikki asked Robin.

"What do I say?" Robin wanted a little guidance at the very least.

"I usually say *hello*. Grace tells me it's wrong. Do what you want I'm not gonna sweat the small stuff, life's too short. I'm not here though." Rikki instructed.

"Rikki Rankin Investigations, this is Robin. How may I help you?" Robin said out of the side of her mouth toward the receiver.

Rikki watched in dismay.

"Hold on I'll ask her," Robin put her hand over the phone.

"I never ever want to see you talk out of the side of your mouth like that! Push the hold button, it's right there." Rikki was laughing at Robin's attempt to answer the phone.

"Shut-up! I want to make sure they hear me. I've never used phones like this. This guy wants to know if you're in. I think he said his name was Owen Kendrick."

Rikki jumped in a circle waving her arms. "I'm not here...I'm on my way to his office. I can't believe you said you'd ask me if I'm here!" Rikki ran to her computer, pulled up a report and printed it off. She stuck it in an envelope and ran toward the back door. "Don't worry about unlocking the front door. Teryn Tennin's going to meet me back here at ten so I'll be back by then." She was out the door.

Robin sat at the desk and looked at the phone. Owen Kendrick was still on hold. She pushed a few buttons trying to get the call off hold. Something happened but she wasn't sure what she did.

"Hello?" Attorney Owen Kendrick said.

"Uuummm, Rikki's on her way to your office." Robin was unsure what to say.

"Okay, is this Grace?"

"No, it's Robin, Rikki's sister."

"Oh, didn't know she had a sister." Owen Kendrick hung up the phone.

"Ugh, what a jerk." Robin hung up the receiver. Her eyes shifted around the empty office. *This is scary.*

*****

On the elevator rising to the ninth floor of a downtown Tulsa high-rise, Rikki began mentally preparing for the interview with Teryn. The elevator stopped at the second floor and the doors opened. Two well-dressed women looked into the elevator and stepped toward the door. One looked at Rikki her eyes widened and jaw dropped. She grabbed the other lady by the arm and stopped her from boarding. Rikki watched as they stood there, dressed to the nines, scared to ride the elevator alone with her, she was amused. Rikki found herself positioned against the sliding elevator door so it wouldn't shut.

"Come on, there's plenty of room." She smiled. *Stupid people afraid I'm going to hurt you, in reality I'd risk my life protecting you.*

"That's okay. Uh, I forgot some documents I need to run back and get." One lady lied.

"Well, Ma'am, see...I know you're lying to me right now... your body language is screaming I'm a liar! Sooo...get on the elevator." She pointed to the inside of the elevator eyes sternly fixed on the women.

"Oh come on, let's just go, we're going to be late." The lady broke loose of her colleague's grasp and entered the elevator. Reluctantly, the liar lady followed.

"Thank you. By the way you looked at me, it seemed like you thought I was going to kill you or something." Rikki was saying as the doors shut and there was no escape for the ladies. She purposely let her jacket open exposing her weapon, in an effort to teach the ladies a lesson. Her intentions were good.

"Actually, it's not you that worries me. It's the people after you." One lady spoke up, huddled with the other lady in the corner of the fear filled elevator.

"Oh didn't you hear? He's dead. Yup, I killed him two days ago." Rikki was nonchalant.

"And he's the only one?"

Rikki laughed, "You're right...probably not." She watched the numbers above the door. "For your own safety ladies, I'd like to offer this advice. If someone tells you to get on an elevator and you are not comfortable with that...turn and walk away, make a scene, do whatever you have to...but don't get on. If I were a psycho killer you'd be on your way to dead right now. You should take a self-defense class or something. Honestly, both of you are perfect targets for the criminals out there." The elevator dinged and doors started to open. "Practice not being victims...have a nice day, ladies." Rikki smiled at them and exited the elevator.

"You're prettier in person!" Liar lady yelled after her. Rikki raised an arm and waved a thank you, she didn't look back.

Grace is right, I have to tell my side. The way the media's been covering this I look like a cold-blooded killer. Rikki was now bothered by the reaction of the ladies in the elevator. She walked into Owen Kendrick's plush office to the reception desk.

Lexi graciously answered the nine blinking phone lines then smiled at Rikki as she hung up with the last caller.

"Hello, Rikki." Lexi was timid and sweet with long black hair. She had a mature demeanor and an old soul, which camouflaged her youth. Plain but naturally cute.

"Hello, you're busy today. I'll just leave this report with you. Will you make sure that Owen gets it?" Rikki smiled at Lexi.

"Well, he really needed to speak with you. Let me tell him you're here." Lexi was always professional.

"No, I really have to go...everything he needs is in the report." Rikki turned to walk out the door. *I have an hour to make it back to the office to meet Teryn, I'm doing good.*

Lexi stood behind the tall marble counter. She removed her earpiece and ran after Rikki. Rikki had reached the elevator dreading the ride down, if it was anything like the ride up. *Who will I scare this time?*

"Rikki? Please speak with Owen. If I let you walk out that door without seeing him, well, I'm afraid he...he will fire me." Lexi hung her head barely glancing up at Rikki.

"Are you serious?"

"Yes. He's not the easiest man to work for. Don't get me wrong, I love my job, he's just hard to understand at times." Lexi said.

"So, are you like totally loyal to this place?" Rikki's wheels were spinning.

"I like what I do just not where I do it." Lexi tried to be polite.

"I'll tell you what, why don't you come to work for me? I've always been impressed with your level of professionalism." Rikki offered.

"Really? Me work for Rikki Rankin Investigations? I don't know if I'm smart enough."

"What? Sure you are. I've seen how you handle things around here and that's exactly what I need. I'll go in there and talk to Owen myself. Can you start today? You can leave with me right now." Rikki applied a little pressure.

"Right now? I'm shocked. I need time to think about this." Lexi let out a squeak of excitement.

"Oh, come on, be spontaneous and follow your gut. You know you want to."

"Oh my gosh! I don't know what to do. I want to say yes but I'm just not sure what I'm saying yes to."

"What does Owen pay you?" Rikki knew how to persuade her.

"I get six dollars and fifty-five cents an hour." Lexi was proud.

"What? That's all he pays you? I'll start you out at eight." Rikki knew Lexi was young and this was probably her first office job.

"Oh my gosh, okay, I'll do it." Lexi was breathing hard now. She waved her hand in front of her face for air.

"You do know it's not gonna to be pretty when I tell Owen I'm stealing you effective immediately. But oh how fun it's gonna be. He is like the biggest jerk ever. Go get your stuff ready and I'm gonna take that report and barge into his office. Let's shake things up around here, shall we?" This was the best idea Rikki had in few days. She was excited about the possibilities.

"Hello, Owen." Rikki barged in his office just as she had planned. Flashed a perfect smile exposing one dimple, "it's a beautiful day, isn't it?" She was a little too perky.

"Hello, Rikki. Aren't you in a good mood today? Guess I thought you'd be somber after killing a man. I wanted to talk to you about what happened with Greg Hayes. You've been all over the news. Have you seen the paper today?"

Rikki hadn't even thought about the paper. "No, I haven't and I don't want to. I also don't want to talk about Greg Hayes. However, there is something I think you should know." She held the report in her hand. "If you want this report you will cut me a check right now. That includes all the back pay. When is your court date on this?" She knew it was the next day.

"I usually pay you after the court date." Owen was confused.

"I know...waaaaay after the court date...I'm not gonna wait three months for payment. I do the work when you need it, so pay me. It's that simple. I know you have the money." She didn't budge.

"I can't just cut you a four thousand dollar check!" Owen argued.

"You can and you will...and it's four thousand, three hundred you owe me. This doesn't have to get ugly Owen, but I'm prepared to do whatever it takes. I've had a bad week, what's one dead attorney added to my list?" Rikki leaned over the desk, in his face. "Get your checkbook." She said slow and clear.

Owen opened the middle drawer on the right side of his desk and pulled out his business checks. He wrote fast, tore out the check and handed it to Rikki.

"Pleasure doing business with you." Rikki smiled as she proofed the check.

"Rikki, you've always been on edge but I've never seen you like this. Are you sure you're alright?" Owen was concerned he didn't want to lose her as an investigator.

"I'm great Owen. I've decided life's too short to put up with all the jerks in the world. So I'm weeding them out of my life...and

Owen...you're one of them. You're rude, you treat people like crap and you never pay me on time." Rikki was matter-of-fact.

"I hope you're going to take some time off. I really think it would do you some good."

Rikki walked toward the door to leave. "By the way, I'm taking Lexi with me. She's tired of your crap too. She's coming to work for me...I offered her more money." Rikki smiled and blinked as if she put a period at the end of the sentence.

"You're lying!" Owen jumped up and followed Rikki down the hall to the reception area.

"Ready?" Rikki said to Lexi.

Lexi had her belongings in hand. "I'm ready!"

"You are serious! Lexi you look scared...is she kidnapping you? Are you going of your own free will?" Owen was shocked.

"Oh good grief, I'm not kidnapping anyone. She chooses to go with me...so back off!" Rikki was ready for confrontation.

"I am scared but she's not making me go." Lexi confessed.

Owen backed off and let them walk out the door. They heard a crash and Rikki turned to look, Owen had thrown the phone down the hall.

"That went well." Rikki smiled at Lexi as they got on the elevator.

Lexi let out a nervous giggle. *What have I gotten myself into?* Fear overtook her. She had just walked out of her job. Now she was befriending the lady who had been all over the news for killing a man. She couldn't deny the excitement she felt along with the fear.

"We have forty minutes to make it back to the office. I have a live interview with Teryn Tennin." Rikki informed her newest employee.

"Seriously? Oh my gosh, what do I need to do? I've never been around anything like that. I knew I wasn't smart enough for this." Lexi's fear got the best of her.

"Calm down. You reek of fear. We've got to work on that! It's no big deal...you won't have to do anything. If I didn't believe that you are perfect for the job I would not have hired you. Believe in yourself a little bit, would you?"

Lexi inhaled deeply through her nose and exhaled slowly through her mouth. "I've just never done anything like this before. Who knew this day would turn out like this?"

Rikki laughed, "I find myself saying that all the time. Just roll with it that's all you can do. Lexi never let people see what's going on inside…always show confidence. That's your first lesson and I'm gonna teach you self-defense ASAP!"

"Now I'm really scared." Lexi wasn't sure she had made the right choice.

Lexi was unaware that her training, Rikki style, had already begun.

Rikki dialed Grace on her cell phone.

"Yes Ma'am." Grace answered.

"Are you gonna be at the office at ten? Teryn is coming for an interview." Rikki jumped right into the conversation.

"I'm already here. Robin was really happy to see me." Grace laughed.

"I bet. Hey, I have a surprise when I get there. You're gonna love this!" Rikki was referring to Lexi. *Grace will be so excited to have an assistant.*

"Great! I have a surprise for you too!" Grace giggled.

4

RIKKI STROLLED INTO THE office with Lexi, ready to spring the surprise on Grace.

"Rikki, it's really you!" A small woman bounced up from the sofa in the lobby and bombarded Rikki. "I have to talk to you! You have to save my life!" The woman rambled holding tightly to a blue gym bag. She wore high-dollar designer clothes and pronounced every syllable in her words with an East Coast accent.

"Surprise!" Grace hollered over the woman with a fake surprised look.

"*A-s-qua-ni-go-hi-s-di* (surprise)!" Rikki hollered back at Grace, pushing Lexi toward her with the same fake surprised look.

Lexi was petrified. The chaos was more than she could endure. Her eyes were bulging, her mouth hung open and her hands were shaking. She felt as if she'd walked into a burning bush with no way out.

Rikki studied Lexi for a second. "Is this you rolling with it?" She whispered to Lexi. Lexi was speechless. "Cause you're sucking at it." Rikki giggled.

"I...I..." Lexi started to stutter.

"Welcome to our world." Rikki smiled and stretched her arms out to each side.

"Excuse me! My life is on the line here! Don't ignore me!" The rich woman was apparently distressed and now angry for not immediately getting Rikki's undivided attention.

"I'm sorry, ma'am. We've just got a lot going on this very moment," Rikki finally addressed the woman.

The front door flew open. Teryn and her crew piled into the office.

"This is too much, I wanna leave but I can't make myself." Robin spoke up as she seated herself in the leather chair for a front row view.

"What is going on here? I have to have your help *now*!" The woman attached herself to Rikki.

"Okay, step into my office." Rikki had to gain control over the chaos. "Lexi see that desk? It's yours. Have a seat and just roll with it for a minute." Rikki winked, trying to ease her nerves. "Everything is going to be just fine." She said to Lexi and the strange woman.

"Her desk? What *is* going on here?" Now Grace was confused.

"I'll get right back to ya on that, Grace." Rikki disappeared into her office with the woman and shut the door.

"Rikki! Are we still going to do the interview?" Teryn yelled after her.

Rikki barely opened the door and yelled through the crack, "give me one second here, Teryn, and I'll be right with you."

The lobby was silent, as everyone wanted to know what was going on in Rikki's office. They strained to hear anything but to no avail, the walls were too thick. Grace knew that it was a losing battle yet she tried along with the rest of them. Who is this woman and what does she want? That was the million-dollar question on everyone's minds.

"Have a seat and try to relax. I promise you, you will be safe in here. As you can see I've got a lot going on at this ten o'clock hour. I would really like to speak with you right now but I have to deal with all these other issues first, then I can fully concentrate on you. Is that fair?" Rikki tried to soothe her, make her feel welcome and understood. "What is your name?"

"That's not important right now." The woman was edgy. She fought the tears but lost the battle. Tears streamed down her face wildly but she still held her lips tight. She dropped her head down allowing her bleached blonde hair to stick to her wet face. "I didn't want to fall apart." She swiped at her hair moving it off her face.

Rikki studied her. *You are going through agony right now.* "It's quite alright. You are in a safe place now so you can fall apart." Rikki handed her a box of Puffs Plus. Rikki knew that whatever she had gone through this lady had held it together and now it was all spilling out.

The woman took the box, used a tissue, and then dug in her gym bag. She rose gracefully, walked up to Rikki's desk and tossed ten stacks of fifty, one hundred-dollar bills down on the desk. "There's fifty thousand dollars. I need your attention right now."

Holy crap, we've got a live one on our hands. Rikki didn't look at the money, instead kept eye contact with the woman. "I wish it were that simple ma'am, I do. But it is going to be at least an hour before I can give you my undivided attention. I feel for what you are going through but I have other pressing obligations that I have to take care of. You are welcome to wait in here or in the lobby. You can leave and come back or just leave and find someone else to help you. It's up to you." Rikki didn't give in to her demand. She wanted to show her that she ran the show and wouldn't be controlled by the almighty dollar.

"I can't leave, I'm lucky I made it here alive. You are the only one who can help me. I'll wait in here, it feels safe." She respected Rikki's way of doing things. She was intrigued that the money didn't faze Rikki. She was used to getting her way, especially when she threw money around.

"It's settled then," Rikki got up and walked toward the door then she abruptly turned around, startling the woman. "You will have to tell me your name sooner or later, but for now I'll give you the house name of Daisy Doe." As Rikki left the room, the woman unknowingly wore a half-cocked smile.

Rikki wanted to speak with Grace immediately when she made eye contact with her; Grace jumped up and walked toward Rikki. Grace knew something juicy had happened by the look on Rikki's face.

"I need to speak with Grace real quick, then I will be with you, Teryn." Rikki said into the air hoping someone heard her. They disappeared into the equipment room.

"That's Lexi from Owen Kendrick's office, right? She works here now?" Grace had many questions.

"Yes and yes. Even better...that woman whom we will call Daisy Doe...yeah...one of those! She threw fifty thousand dollars on my desk just now." Rikki couldn't get it out fast enough. Grace knew what Daisy Doe meant.

"No way! Fifty thousand dollars?" Grace was intrigued.

"Oh yes way! For some reason she doesn't want to give us her name. So get her a *special* drink. I think there are drinks in the fridge left over from the I-killed-a-man party. The timing on this one really sucks!" Rikki had just told Grace to get her fingerprints and find out anything and everything she could on this woman.

"Okay, I'll go ask her what she would like to drink. Should I break Lexi in right? Have her come with me?" Grace liked the idea.

"Sure, since I hired her to be your assistant." Rikki smiled still not accepting Grace's resignation.

"Oh, that was thoughtful, since I don't work here anymore." Grace confirmed her resignation.

"*Wii* (yes) you do, you are just taking some time off." Rikki fluffed her hair, freshened her lips and straightened her clothes. "Am I camera ready?" She had to switch gears fast.

"Simply gorgeous." Grace sarcastically acknowledged.

"Get the prints, send 'em to Deputy Thames and have him run 'em. Then we will do a thorough background. By the way, we need to get this done within the hour. I'd like you to be on air with me...I know people would like to hear from you too. So as soon as you shoot those prints off to Deputy Thames just get in eyesight of me and I'll bring you in on the interview. Sound like a plan?" Rikki tried to stomp out all the fires at once.

"Sounds good...also sounds like I still work here." Grace spun around to the door.

"Dang it, Grace, you aren't quitting so just stop it!" Rikki wanted things back to normal.

Who does she think she is? Ticks me off she knows I won't quit. "You're a stubborn mule! If you didn't need me so much, I would just walk away." She opened the door and walked out.

Rikki smiled ear to ear. *What a relief that is to hear.* "You're right. I do need you and I admit it." She followed Grace out the door. They had on their game faces, ready to conquer all that waited for them in the other part of the office.

Teryn and her crew were set-up and ready to roll.

Robin sat in the leather chair with her legs crossed, swinging the top one nervously. Her eyes were squinted as she studied Lexi, Teryn and the cameraman. It appeared that she was giving them all a wicked look, ready to pounce on them at any moment.

Grace approached Lexi's desk. "Welcome aboard, Lexi. Come with me and I'll show you a few things. First thing you should know...things can change minute by minute around here so be ready for anything." Grace put it gently.

"Grace, who's that lady? She's been giving me a nasty look." Lexi was leery.

"That's Robin, Rikki's sister. It's not intentional. Once you get to know her you'll love her. Rikki gets the same look sometimes. Come to think of it, so does their Dad. Must be that Indian thing." Grace soothed Lexi's nerves.

"Okay, as long as she's harmless. Well, I'm ready to dive in and learn everything I can. I can't believe I'm actually here. You know, when you or Rikki would come into Owen's office I always thought you guys were so intimidating and led such an exciting life." Lexi was eager.

"Exciting yes, glamorous...not so much. Don't be misled."

"Um, Rikki's doing a live interview on TV, she bullied Owen into paying her four thousand three hundred dollars, and she talked me into leaving with her...that's all before ten o'clock. Never a dull moment from where I'm sitting. It does appear glamorous from the outside." Lexi admitted.

"She forgot to tell me about the money she got from Owen. Yes, I guess I've just been here too long...seems normal to me." Grace admitted. "Okay, most important thing that we cannot, and will not, waiver on is confidentiality. No matter what happens you cannot talk about it, reveal names or speak to the press... nothing. HIPAA has nothing on what we expect in that area. Best practice is not to say anything about anything to anybody."

"Okay, I get it." Lexi said.

"Good. Next thing, when you answer the phone don't say your name, don't give out any information whatsoever. Just say investigations or agency, something like that. No names, nothing informative." Grace instructed.

"Got it." Lexi answered.

"You must learn to roll with things. Watch for the smallest details. This leads me to our mission at hand. Just follow me and be friendly. Don't show your nerves and don't act surprised about anything."

"Okay. Are you going to tell me what the mission is?" Lexi asked.

"We are going to introduce ourselves to the strange lady in Rikki's office. Be gracious and make sure she's comfortable." Grace held back details.

"Okay, I can handle that." Lexi was relieved that it was something simple.

They walked into Rikki's office graciously. "Hello, I'm Grace and this is Lexi."

"Hello." Lexi offered.

"Hi." The woman didn't offer anything else.

"Do you need something to drink or anything else at all?" Grace smiled.

"Something to drink would be great. I'm parched."

"What would you like? I think we have a little of everything."

"Diet Pepsi?" The woman asked.

"That we can handle." Grace and Lexi left.

In the kitchen Grace carefully washed and wiped down a glass. She skillfully handled the glass with a towel making sure not to get her prints on it. She filled the glass with ice then filled it with Diet Pepsi. She picked it up with the towel and placed it on the palm of her hand.

Lexi watched Grace. "Is there a reason you're doing what you're doing?" She was scared of the answer but figured it would be better to know.

"Well, as a matter a fact there is. If she doesn't want to tell us her name, we figure it out on our own." Grace said.

"Oh my gawd, you can do that?" Lexi was shocked. "Did you see all that money on the desk? What was that about?" Lexi was shocked but did her best to roll with it.

"Yes, we can do that and you are going to learn how. I did see the money. Evidently that's what she wants to pay Rikki to do whatever it is she needs." Grace whispered. "Come on, we're on a timeline here."

"Okay, what do I need to do?" Lexi was really getting into things now.

"Just be friendly and don't show any emotion." Grace reiterated.

"Okay. Hey, at some point I need to call my boyfriend and tell him where he needs to pick me up because he has my car." Lexi remembered.

"Oh sure, feel free to use the phones anytime. And I should warn you that lines one and two are bugged. Use line three for personal calls. We record all the calls on the first two lines. It really does come in handy. You'll see." Grace revealed more details about Lexi's new job.

Lexi's eyes were big. The mere thought of the lines being bugged seemed scary. "I'll keep that in mind."

"Game face on! No emotion." Grace saw the deer in the headlights look on Lexi. "Will you open the door?"

Lexi dropped her head trying to get her game face on. She was learning quickly. She let out a breath and opened the door with a smile.

Without hesitation Daisy Doe grabbed the glass of Diet Pepsi and guzzled it down. She looked at Grace a little embarrassed of the gulping sounds that had come from her throat.

"Wow, you were thirsty. Guess you've had a pretty rough day." Grace commented.

"It's been a rough three days. I can't even remember the last time I ate." Daisy Doe felt more comfortable and divulged a small amount of information.

"Did you want more Diet Pepsi? How about something to snack on? We have chips and stuff." Grace offered as Daisy Doe sat the glass back on the palm of her hand.

"Yes, please, that sounds great. Thank you for making me feel so comfortable." She answered.

"No problem. Thanks for being patient with Rikki. She has a lot on her plate right now." Lexi got in on the conversation. She followed Grace to the door. "We'll be right back with food and drinks," she smiled and shut the door.

"That was very good, Lexi. You're going to do just fine." Grace acknowledged.

In the kitchen Grace grabbed a new glass filled it up with Diet Pepsi then filled a plate with veggies, chips, fruit and dip. They dropped it off to Daisy Doe then got down to business.

Lexi's first experience in the equipment room was enlightening to say the least. She was fascinated with all the equipment as she watched Grace skillfully pull the fingerprints off the glass and scanned the image into the computer. The image appeared on the computer screen and Grace picked up her cell phone.

"Deputy Thames? It's Grace. I'm doing good, the initial shock of it all is wearing off and I'm back to business as usual. Which brings me to why I'm calling. I'm going to e-mail you a set of fingerprints. Do you have time to run them now? Rikki needs this ASAP." Grace paused as Deputy Thames answered.

Lexi was hearing only one side of the conversation and was impressed that with just a phone call the fingerprints were going to be run through the law enforcement database. *I think I'm going to like it here.* She smiled.

"That's great! Yes, we do need to get together. You can buy us dinner. Thanks." Grace hung up the phone. She turned to Lexi. "And that is it...we should have the results in less than thirty minutes. Now, I need to go out and do the interview with Rikki." Grace bent over and shook her hair then flipped it back. She checked her face, made some minor adjustments and went out to the lobby for the second phase of the plan.

Teryn was asking Rikki questions as Grace positioned herself behind the camera, in front of Rikki. It took Rikki two seconds to get Grace in front of the camera.

"That is just tragic. You and Grace are very lucky to have gotten out unharmed." Teryn said.

"We are very thankful and blessed. Right Grace? *Ga-lu-tsv* (come)," Rikki motioned for Grace to sit with her on the leather sofa.

Grace situated herself on the sofa as the cameraman attached a mic to her collar.

"So glad you could join us, Grace." Teryn welcomed her.

"Thank you and thank you to all the people that have shown their support, it means a lot." Grace said. "The initial shock is wearing off and we will be back to business probably sooner than we had originally thought," she smiled at the camera. *Especially with fifty thousand dollars lying on Rikki's desk.*

"Grace, can you tell us about the seven deadbolts on the front door?" Teryn had always thought that was over the top but never had the guts to ask.

"Safety in numbers, Teryn." Grace answered without giving out any details to how it all worked and changed everyday.

"You have a..." Teryn was cut-off.

The front door was shoved open and a big burly man abruptly entered. "Where is she?" He looked around the room, ignorant that the camera was aimed at him and rolling.

"Stranger danger!" Grace yelled, without thinking about being live on air. She looked down, closed her eyes and tried not to laugh. Rikki turned her head to the side away from Grace and smirked, trying not to laugh as well.

Rikki stood up calmly and walked over to Lexi's desk where she sat with her heart pounding out of her chest. "Go in my office and lock the door...have Daisy Doe look out the blinds and see if she's seen this guy before then call Grace's cell." She whispered to Lexi.

Lexi moved nonchalantly and Rikki approached the man. "Sir, can I help you? This is my office you just barged into." Rikki flashed a smile.

"Are you getting this?" Teryn whispered to the cameraman.

He nodded as he held the camera that was feeding a live television broadcast.

Grace watched Rikki. *Oh wow, he's gonna to get his butt kicked.*

Grace's cell phone rang. She flipped it open but didn't say anything. Rikki watched Grace for a second. Grace nodded her head at Rikki. *Daisy Doe has seen him before.*

"Where is the woman that drives that white Mercedes?" He seemed frantic and jumpy.

"No one in here drives a white Mercedes. A lady walked through earlier, she went out the back door. Come on I'll show you." Rikki flat out lied.

They walked side by side down the hall to the back of the office. Rikki stuck her right hand under her jacket and released her gun from the holster, holding it under her jacket.

"This woman, is she in trouble?" Rikki made conversation.

He didn't answer.

"Strong, silent type?" Rikki mocked him. *Nu-da-nv-dv-na a-s-ga-ya* (crazy man).

The man's right arm flew up and hit Rikki in the left shoulder, spinning her sideways. He forced her against the wall with his left forearm thrust against her throat.

Oh you started it now buddy! Rikki's knee rammed into his groin, and then she shoved him with her left hand, against the wall on the other side of the hallway. The 9mm pistol pressed against his head with reckless speed.

He swung at Rikki with his right hand; Rikki blocked it with her left. He followed through with a right uppercut under Rikki's arm that held the gun to his head. His fist connected, busting Rikki's bottom lip. Blood spewed onto Rikki's black leather jacket and off white tank top.

"Oh, you'll be sorry you did that, you sorry excuse for a man!" Without hesitation Rikki spun him around with the weight of her body and pressed him face first into the wall. Her gun pressed into his back with her right hand, she patted him down with the left hand.

"Rikki!" Robin yelled trying to get by the cameraman in the hallway to help her sister, everything was happening so fast.

"Don't touch my gun!" The man was packing a .45 semi-automatic—in other words—a small cannon. Rikki quickly removed and tossed it down the hall. The revolver landed at the feet of the cameraman. Rikki spun him back around throwing her elbow into his face and causing his nose to bleed. That wasn't good enough. She kneed his groin two times as fast as she could and then knocked him out with one blow to the head with the butt of her gun. She watched as he slid down the wall and slumped on the floor. That was her signal that she could stop fighting.

"That's okay I got it!" Rikki looked at the cameraman standing there watching the fight through his camera lens. She was trying to see her sister when she realized she was live on TV. "Could someone call 911?" She said into the camera with blood dripping down her chin.

The camera pointed to Teryn. "And that is a day in the life of Rikki and Grace." She wrapped up the story with Rikki in the background handcuffing the lifeless man lying in the hallway. Grace stood watching with the phone up to her ear.

Before Rikki released him to Officer Stone Russell she confiscated his cell phone, slipping it to Grace who then slipped it into her pocket.

Officer Stone Russell loaded the man into his patrol car and shut the door. "Rikki, we're gonna leave an officer here just to make it easier for us, seems like we are running back and forth between your office and the station. But at least you didn't shoot this one." Officer Russell teased.

"Shut-up! That almost hurt my feelings. Hey, Stone, I really wanna talk to this guy...or you can find out who he is and what he wants with my client." Rikki leaned against the patrol car.

"I'll find out what I can and let ya know. Stay out of trouble." He leaned in and hugged Rikki, leaving a gentle kiss on her cheek.

"I'll do my best, but trouble keeps finding me!" She hugged him back and it felt better than it should. It was no secret the pair briefly dated a couple of years previous. For Rikki he was Mr. Right-now, not Mr. Right—just like the rest of her men.

5

GRACE HUNG UP THE phone and disappeared into the equipment room. Deputy Thames got a hit on the fingerprints. Grace went to work, bouncing from one computer to the next, running the name through all the databases, and printing every piece of information she could find.

Robin sat with Rikki on the sofa holding an ice-filled rag on her busted bottom lip. Rikki was silent, contemplating her next move, ignoring the throbbing sensation of her mouth.

Lexi sat in shock at the morning's events. It was the first day on her new job. Part of her wanted to get up and run, while another part of her didn't want to miss a thing. She decided to call her boyfriend and break the news that she is now part of Rikki Rankin Investigations.

"*What*? That chick that's been on the news for killing that dude? You work for her? You got to be kidding me. Tell me this is a joke." Lexi's boyfriend responded to the news.

"I'm not joking. Oh no, let me call you back!" Lexi hung up the phone. She picked up line three to call him back.

"Why'd you hang up on me?" He said when he answered the phone.

"I forgot lines one and two are bugged. I'm supposed to use line three for personal calls."

"No way! You cannot work there. It's too dangerous. Lexi, I just saw her on TV beating a man down. That Grace chick just stood there talking on her cell phone, like no big deal."

"Oh, you saw that? That guy attacked her so she had to defend herself. She started me out at eight dollars an hour." Lexi defended Rikki.

"Really, eight dollars? Yeah but people want her dead. It's not worth it." He argued.

"It's not that bad. I'm learning how to roll with things. I've already learned things I'd never dreamed possible. Just come and pick me up here and you can meet Rikki and Grace. I know you'll like them." She stood her ground, something new for her.

"Guess I don't have a choice. Bye." He didn't like her newfound confidence.

Grace stuck her head out of the equipment room door. "Rikki?"

Rikki slung the ice filled rag off her mouth then jumped up and disappeared into the equipment room with Grace.

"So here's what we know. Her name is Jade Brackin, always been an upstanding citizen, one record seven years ago for speeding...that's it. She's married, no children, very wealthy and does lots of charity work. I found these articles about her and the work she does," Grace handed Rikki the articles and continued to brief her on the case. "She's from Niagara Falls, New York. Three days ago she was accused of murdering her brother-in-law. She disappeared and, of course, we know where she ended up. One strange thing though, she was here in Tulsa and flew back the day before he was murdered. That's all we got." She handed Rikki the articles about the murder.

Rikki's lip was numb and swollen. "Thasss goo' wo'k." She sounded like a child learning to talk. "Will you caw 'tone see wha' he gaw on 'tranger danger?" Rikki laughed deep in her throat at Grace hollering stranger danger.

Grace laughed when she figured out what Rikki meant. "I know 'stranger danger' just flew out of my mouth right on TV. I wanted to crawl under the desk...isn't that what second graders do? Holler 'stranger danger'?" Grace laughed at herself. "I'll call Stone. You need to thaw out your mouth so you can talk!"

Rikki went into the bathroom to rinse her mouth out. She spit blood into the sink and looked in the mirror at her busted, swollen lip that was now turning purple. *This is just great. Mind over matter, I'm not in e-hi-s-dv* (pain), Rikki repeated to herself so she could concentrate on interviewing Jade Brackin.

Rikki walked down the hall to her office. She overheard Lexi on the phone. "I'm so sorry but we have no comment. I'll let her know you called." Lexi hung up the phone and picked up the next ringing line. Rikki smiled, *hiring her was a great idea.*

Rikki stood in front of Lexi's desk, "I'm going to give you a raise. You now make ten dollars an hour," she turned and walked away.

Rikki paused briefly at her office door, taking a moment to draw in a deep breath and to whisper a short prayer. *Thank you for an open mind to hear things not even said. Keep me focused and shine through me that I can help this woman. Lord, protect Grace, Lexi, me and our families as I do what it takes with no fear to solve this murder. Amen.*

Feeling peaceful and confident Rikki opened the door to her office. She found Daisy Doe pacing back and forth, on the verge of a nervous breakdown.

"Thank God you are finally back!" She noticed Rikki's face. "Ouch! What happened to your lip?"

"Got in a little scuffle with your friend. Let's start with him. You have my undivided attention now. How do you know this guy?" Rikki didn't have time for small talk and wasn't good at it anyway.

"I don't know him, I've only seen him. He followed me from New York. I tried to ditch him several times but he always seems to find me. I think he's been following me for four or five days now. I don't know, my days are running together...but I swear he was trying to kill me." She took a breath.

"I doubt he was trying to kill you or he would have...did you notice anyone else following you?"

"I'm not sure. I've been so paranoid I thought everyone that made eye contact was trying to kill me." She finally sat down on the sofa in Rikki's office and crossed her legs. "I'm exhausted. I can't go on like this." She broke down in tears.

Rikki was silent, an interrogation technique she had learned years ago. Makes the other person feel obligated to keep talking. She touched her lip, *yup still swollen.* Then she chose to get some things clear with Daisy Doe.

"I can promise you this. I will get you to a safe-house while I investigate whatever it is you want me to investigate," as if she didn't know, "but you have to hang tough, never give up, and trust me with your life. Straight up honesty, no bull crap. Can you do that?"

"I don't feel like I have a choice, so yes I can do that." Daisy Doe felt at ease whenever Rikki was around. "Your lip looks terrible, I'm really sorry about that."

"Don't worry about it, not your fault. Believe me I've had worse. Let's get started...I need you to start from the beginning and tell me why you're here." Rikki leaned back in her chair and plopped her cowboy boots on the top of her desk. As she did she hit the record button on a recorder mounted under the desk across from the Colt Detective Special .38 snub-nosed revolver, which was mounted on the right. She didn't always tell the other person they were being recorded. She knew from experience that people clam up when there's a recording device in plain view.

"There's not much to tell really. My brother-in-law was murdered three days ago and I'm being accused. I didn't do it. I need someone who can prove I didn't do it, that's why I came to you. I know you were accused of murder several months ago and you were able to prove who did it and clear your name."

"You pretty much started at the end. I need you to start from the beginning." Rikki was blunt. "Every detail including names" she was ready to take notes with her fifty-cent ballpoint pen pressed on a legal pad.

"My sister, Lyric Casteel, and her husband, Miles Casteel, have been married for seventeen years. Not happily either. I guess they stayed together because of money. Millions. My sister and I are total opposites. She's very greedy, materialistic even. Miles always hated that about her, everything is for show. She has to have it all. I bet she can spend twenty thousand dollars in a day." Daisy Doe paused and sipped from her glass of Diet Pepsi. "Is any of this relevant? I don't want to waste time talking about things that doesn't matter."

"The more I know...the better. Keep blabbing." Rikki didn't look up from her notes.

"Okay. Um, well, I seem to get along better with Miles than I do my own sister. Miles and I should've been brother and sister instead of Lyric being my sister."

"How 'bout husband and wife?" Rikki interrupted her.

"Excuse me?" Daisy Doe was appalled by the accusation.

"You and Miles, husband and wife...does that seem so farfetched to you?" Rikki looked up to watch her reaction.

Daisy Doe's eyes shot to the floor and widened, lips tightened and thinned. "I don't know what to say," she looked up and made eye contact with Rikki. "Yes, that seems very farfetched." Her eyes glanced to the left.

Rikki watched Jade's body language scream liar. "I think you had an affair with Miles." She had to push the issue farther. Frankly, Rikki got off confronting a liar. It's not what they say, it's how they say and react to it.

No response from Daisy Doe. Rikki waited patiently, depending on her 'be silent' theory. She made notes on the legal pad and tapped her pen on the desk a few times before setting it down. After a moment, Rikki leaned back in her chair and clasped her hands behind her head, all the while staring intently at Daisy Doe. Several minutes ticked by.

Obviously uncomfortable, and more than a little embarrassed, she finally asked Rikki "Why do you assume that?"

Rikki only shrugged her shoulders and remained silent, her dark eyes never wavering as she continued to watch her client closely. She imagined what her lip looked like by now. It felt puffy. She licked it and used her upper lip to measure just how puffy it was. *A-yo* (ouch)! *That sucker's sore!* Her thoughts were drifting. *I need to go workout. Wonder what Jaxon's doing...no I don't... okay, yes I do. Focus on Daisy Doe...hell I know her name is Jade Brackin...think I'll throw that out there.*

"Daisy Doe, let's get real, shall we?" Rikki stood up and paced the floor. She wanted to jump out of her own skin. One symptom of her ADHD, time for a Ritalin pill, she hadn't taken one in who knows how long. "Your name is Jade Brackin. You banged your brother-in-law. Your sister knows you did her husband but she really don't care. She loves his money and you love him. Am I getting closer to the real story here?"

Some kind of squeak seeped out of Jade. *Did Miss High and Mighty just fart?* Rikki couldn't help but giggle to herself. She looked away to hide her smirk. *Should I fart to make her feel more comfortable?* Rikki lost it and started laughing at the mere thought of it all. The more she tried not to laugh the more her whole body shook. *I gotta get outta here for a second.*

"I'll be right back," Rikki hurried out of her office.

"Omigod, what have you done?" Grace was afraid to ask. The sight of Rikki laughing until tears rolled down her cheeks was always good cause for alarm. They called it the 'ugly laugh'.

"I don't know what's wrong with me! Jade is going to think I'm outta my mind! She made a squeak when I told her I suspect she banged her brother-in-law...for a second I thought she farted... and it just cracked me up." Rikki still tried to gain control of her laughter.

"No, you didn't!" Grace couldn't help but laugh along with Rikki even though she didn't want too. "You ain't right, Rikki! Get control of yourself...I know what it is...you need a Ritalin pill." Grace disappeared.

Lexi sat at her desk laughing along with Rikki. She had never been around anything like this before. "Honestly, I don't know what to think," Lexi managed to say. "The beating of a man in the hallway, the TV cameras, the secret fingerprinting, and now the banging and the farting. This is all before noon. And then you guys tell me I can't talk about any of this...well, no one would believe me anyway." Lexi put her head down on her desk then she barely raised it. "I'll tell you this, I love my job already."

Grace returned with a glass of water and a pill. "Take this, get your game face on and get in there and take care of business! Times a wastin' and we need to figure out what we are gonna do with her. You do have a bounty waiting and another case to finish." Grace always got Rikki back on track.

Rikki took the Ritalin with a gulp of water. "You're right. I'm on it. It's just been a hell of a day. How's my lip? Feels real poofy," she handed the glass to Grace and walked back in her office. When the door shut behind her, Grace and Lexi busted a gut laughing. Grace just shook her head and rolled her eyes.

"See, I told you things change from minute to minute around here." Grace made her point. "You can help me with one thing. If Rikki seems over-the-top hyper or she's having six conversations at the same time, jumping from one subject to another, or asks a question then walks off before you can answer, like she did just now, causally ask her if she's taken her meds. She won't if we don't remind her. Trust me she will wear you out."

"Okay, I'll try. I would've never thought you guys were like this." Lexi was getting a clearer picture of Rikki and Grace.

"Trust me, you have no idea," Grace walked back to her office.

Rikki settled back down behind her desk. "I'm really sorry, Jade. It's just been a heck of a week. Where were we?" Rikki cleared her throat.

"You were telling me how I...how did you put it? Banged my brother-in-law," Jade stopped speaking and raised her hands. "Wait. Before we go any farther I'd like to know what you were laughing about."

"Oh, really, it was nothing. I think everything is starting to get to me a little bit. Did you know I shot a man two days ago? Killed him. He was going to shoot me and Grace both so I had to do it." Rikki opened up to her hoping to gain her trust. Maybe if she tried harder to be more personable Jade would be able to talk to her easier.

"I did see that on like four different channels, in three different states. It was shocking news for me when I first heard about it. I was on my way here to meet you and you were all over the news." Jade was glad they talked about that even if it was brief. "Must have been seven years ago when Miles and I had an affair. It was short-lived but intense. Lyric and I didn't even get along when we were kids. My family comes from old oil and gas money so we never had to earn anything. I began charity work when I was fifteen and Lyric would make fun of me. She would say "why do you like helping those poor people anyway?" She's very selfish."

"So she didn't marry Miles for his money?" Rikki tried to get the whole picture.

"Well, yes, in a way. She would never marry anyone that wasn't already rich. She won't share her money but sure does take his money. Miles buys and sells companies but he made his millions on the stock market years ago, he earned every penny of his money." The corners of her lips curled up at the thought of Miles being a hard worker. "That's attractive, don't you agree?"

Rikki smiled. *Having a job and a car is attractive.* "Yes that's very attractive. It's so attractive, in fact, I'd wanna say, throw me down and pull my hair a little bit." She laughed.

"I've never heard anything like that before in my life. You sure know how to throw the shock into a person." Jade tried to lighten up, but she was raised prim and proper, including charm school. Ladies didn't even think things like that; much less say it out loud. "You are a gorgeous lady, like a porcelain doll, but the things that come out of your mouth! Oh, my heavens!"

"I arrest bad guys for a living. I hang out with cops and a variety of other law enforcement agents. I'm not prim and proper! Lucky for you though, right?" Rikki felt like Mary Poppins had just scolded her.

"I'm not judging you at all. In fact I wish I could be a tiny bit more like that. Say what's on my mind." Jade confessed.

"Well, why don't you give it a whirl, right now? Tell me what's on your mind about all this you're going through."

"It's crap! I didn't kill Miles, I loved him! Oh, that felt good. It wouldn't surprise me if my sister didn't do it just to get his money." She put her hands over her mouth at the sound of what she had said. "It's true though!" Muffled through her fingers.

"So you think your sister did this for the money?" Rikki was finally getting what she wanted. She had that special gift that brought the worst out in folks.

"I don't know. I guess it wouldn't surprise me. Miles told me about four months ago that Lyric had spent so much of her money that he didn't think she had much left. She was really nervous about it. He also gave me this." She reached into her gym bag and pulled out a large envelope and handed it to Rikki. It was sealed and wrinkled.

"Do you know what's in here?" Rikki waved it in the air.

"No. I haven't opened it. Miles said to open it if anything happened to him. At the time I didn't think anything would ever happen to him. Now I can't bring myself to open it. So feel free to rip it open." Jade fought the tears again.

Rikki already had it open before Jade even finished the sentence. She pulled out a legal document. She looked it over without saying a word. Curiosity was killing Jade. After carrying the envelope for four months all of a sudden she had to know what was inside. She tried to be patient. She tried to read Rikki's face as to what it was. Rikki didn't have an expression, but undoubtedly her brain was running a mile a minute.

"I can't stand it! What is it?" Jade finally asked.

"It's a will. Seems you are a very rich woman. Which also means law dogs will see this as a motive. Good news, bad news kinda deal." Rikki answered without looking away from the will. She believed Jade had not opened the envelope and really didn't know what was inside. Would anyone else believe that though?

"What do you mean? I'm already a rich woman."

"Miles left everything to you...everything. Lyric is not even mentioned in this will. This was written in June. The attorney is Gates Linvick. Do you know him?" Rikki was surprised that

Miles didn't leave his wife a dime. *Guess there really was trouble in paradise.*

"Gates Linvick has been Miles' attorney for years. They were best friends in college and are to this day...or you know what I mean...until Miles died."

"We need to find out when they are gonna read the will. I bet your sister doesn't know about this and, if she does, maybe it made her so mad she had him removed from earth. How was he murdered?" Rikki was ready to get into the particulars of the murder.

"He was shot...in the heart." Jade had tears rolling down her cheeks. "I've never even held a gun. How could anyone actually believe that I could have committed such a crime?" Rikki handed her more Puffs Plus.

"Jade, I know this is hard for you but you have to tell me everything. We are just getting into the rough stuff. Where was he when he was shot?" Rikki continued questioning her.

"You don't know? He was here in Tulsa at a hotel downtown. He was here on business. It's been all over the news right along with you. Ironic I guess." Jade answered.

I should've known that, if I'd read those articles Grace gave me. "Wow! I haven't watched the news in over a week. Especially the last few days, I hate to see myself on TV. That's good news though. I have more contacts here. Where were you?" *Uh-huh, that's what you were doing in Tulsa before the murder.* Rikki was relieved that she didn't have to go to New York to investigate the murder.

Jade didn't answer Rikki's question right away. She sat silently on the couch holding a tear drenched Puffs Plus and staring at the floor. Any sympathy Rikki had for Jade dissipated. *What reason would she have to lie to me, or hold back important details? I think I made it pretty clear to be honest.* Rikki remained silent, shaking her foot and getting more agitated by the second. *I'm not taking this case. I can't help her if she's a liar...a rich liar, but still a liar.* She picked up the Last Will and Testament and began to slide it back into the envelope when she discovered there was another piece of paper still inside. She glanced at Jade and slid the paper out of the envelope. Gently unfolding it to minimize the crinkling of the paper, she began reading a letter from the dead man, Miles Casteel.

Jade, My Dearest Love,

You made my life worth living. I cherished every moment we shared together, darling. You reading this can only mean one thing, they finally got me. In June of 2008 I changed my will, leaving everything to you, my one true love.

You should know that your sister is totally broke. I suspect that she has been blackmailed for several years. You can always call upon Gates if you need help. He is the only other person that knows about the changing of the will.

I must warn you to watch out for yourself. I've incurred such harassment the last few months and I don't want you to be the next victim. I don't mean to scare you, love, but I also want you safe. I will be waiting at heaven's door to greet you some sweet day.

All my love is yours darling,

Miles

Jade still gazed at the floor. *There's a motive, his wife's in the poor house.* Rikki wondered what was going through her head. Rikki walked out of her office with the letter and will in hand, without saying a word to Jade. She went straight to the copier and made a copy of the documents. She wasn't even sure if she was going to take the case. But the fifty thousand dollars on her desk persuaded her otherwise.

Back at her desk, Rikki's patience had dissolved and turned to hostility. She wanted to pick Jade up and shake her until she told the truth, the whole truth and nothing but the truth. *So help me God, don't let me harm her.* Rikki fought the urge. The fifty thousand dollars sat blaring at her on the desk. One fast and forceful shove and the money landed on the floor. *That felt good! I wanna do it again...*everything boiling inside Rikki the past few days had made its way to the surface. She stood up wanting something else to shove around. The envelope with the will and letter sat on the desk. She picked it up and threw it more at Jade than to her.

"Get your money and get out!" Rikki yelled raged with anger.

"You're not going to help me?" Jade said overcome with fright.

"I can't help you. You're a liar. Nothin' I can do." The fury leaping off of Rikki's face was fearsome enough but the tone in her voice made Jade want to hide under the desk. Rikki had to get a grip on herself. She stormed out of her office and slammed the door.

Rikki fled to the kitchen. As soon as she went through the door her fists were flying in the air, followed by a few roundhouse karate kicks. The room was blurry and Rikki's teeth were clenched and grinding. She wanted to explode, scream as loud as she could.

Grace heard the door slam and saw Rikki flicker through the hall by her office. She followed her to the kitchen and stood in the doorway with her arms folded and observed Rikki's fit of anger. It wasn't the first time Grace had witnessed such a fit, but it had been awhile. This fit seemed to have much more fire behind it though. *Wow, that's some pinned up aggression right there. Wish I could do that.* Grace considered joining Rikki in the tantrum. All of the sudden, Rikki just stopped. Her jaw muscles flexed and nostrils flared as she rapidly sucked air in and out. She saw Grace but couldn't make out who was there because the room was still blurry. Rikki backed up until she hit the counter then she leaned on it until her vision cleared.

"Feel better?" Grace finally asked.

"Yup." Rikki caught her breath, "I don't like to be lied too. Did she leave?"

"I know you don't. No, she's still here." Grace paused. "Whatcha gonna do?"

"I wanna go work out. I have so much I need to do. I'm not sure if I want this case or not. If she were more cooperative I would, but I'm not gonna make her tell me the truth. Hell, she probably did it and wants me to make her look innocent and pin it on someone else." She answered. "What do you think?"

Grace pondered the question for a moment. "I think we've been through hell the last few days. I think we need a little time away to clear our heads and relax but I don't think that's gonna happen. I think you've probably scared Jade to death by now and she may never speak to another human being. I think we should talk to her together...good cop, bad cop...I think I'm the good cop. I think you would be sorry if you didn't take this case and something bad happened to that woman sitting in your office. I think I know how you are. I think she really needs our help. I think you were laughing hysterically thirty minutes ago and now you are in a fit of rage...that's just weird. I think..."

"Okay, shut-up already. Dang." Rikki interrupted Grace's "I think" moment.

"I was going to say, I think your lip is bleeding." Grace turned and left the kitchen.

"Oh, crap." Rikki touched her swollen lip—it was bleeding again. She spit into the kitchen sink, and turned on the water to rinse it out. *I've got to calm down. I'll talk to Jade one more time but if she doesn't cooperate, that's it. I need to search her car for bugs...I'm sure someone put a tracking device on it.* Rikki watched the bloody water spin down the drain.

6

GRACE STEPPED INTO RIKKI'S office to check on Jade. She sat on the sofa traumatized. Grace caught the same expression when she saw the fifty thousand dollars scattered all over the floor.

"She threw this at me and yelled," Jade said holding up the envelope. "I know I should leave but I have nowhere to go."

"Everything's gonna be all right," Grace sat down beside Jade. "Rikki's debuggin' your car right now. She's calmed down some. You must think we're a crazy bunch of hillbillies." Grace smiled.

"No, I don't. Tragedy has touched us all this week. I think we are all doing very well, considering." Jade smiled back at Grace. They had an understanding.

Rikki walked to the mall behind her office. She canvassed the area for anyone that could possibly be watching Jade. From inside the upscale clothing store, *Every Access,* she analyzed the parking lot and a gas station across the street. There didn't seem to be any suspicious vehicles.

"I'm stressed." Kam, the storeowner, said standing behind Rikki.

"Why are you stressed little Kammy?" Rikki asked.

"Cuz you're in my store and people want to kill you." Kam held a piece of her long blonde hair and twirled it through her fingers.

She camouflaged her head in a rack of clothing, to conceal her identity while she spoke with Rikki.

Rikki pivoted, to face Kam. "I just wanted to refresh my inner rock star." "Refresh your inner rock star" is the store's slogan. "I'll go out your back door. I can't have you being stressed...cute britches, how much?" Rikki strolled through the store with Kam on her heels.

"I'm sorry Rikki but you know how I am. I'd have a panic attack and die if I even saw a gun. And those jeans are two hundred fifteen dollars." Kam spoke fast and grabbed short breaths between words.

"Hi, how are you?" Rikki said to a customer that was gawking at her. "Calm down, Kammy, everything is fine. Take long deep breaths or you're gonna need a brown bag to breathe in. Call me if you need anything," Rikki exited through the back door.

"I will. Thanks, Rikki." Kam shut the door and locked it. She only went back to make sure it was locked six times in the next hour.

Rikki's observation of the surroundings was up to snuff, nothing out of the ordinary. She entered through the back door of her office, straight to the equipment room, then out the front door to debug Jade's car. In her haste to accomplish the mission, Rikki didn't even pause to speak to Lexi as she darted past her desk.

Straight away, Rikki found a Protrak Ranger tracking device under Jade's car. This device is monitored through the internet, as close to real time as you can get. A laptop is all someone would need to track Jade's every move within seconds. *I can't wait to call Stone and see what he's found out about Stranger Danger. I just bet this belongs to him.* She removed the device from Jade's car.

The debugging equipment was still blinking as Rikki waved it beside the car. She removed the battery from the Protrak Ranger, still blinking. *There has to be another bug on this car.* Now, on her back under the car, she searched for another tracking device. She spent at least fifteen minutes under the car, focused on one small greasy area at a time.

"There you are!" Rikki got excited when she spotted the device. "Two devices, two stalkers? I think I'll need more than fifty thousand dollars for this one." Rikki talked to herself as she crawled out from under the car. Positioned on the pavement beside Jade's car, with her legs crossed, Indian style she studied the second tracking device. "This is a T-Track System. Wow...we've got a problem. Why are two people tracking Jade Brackin?" She removed the battery from the device. On all fours, she crawled around the car and waved the wand, to make sure there wasn't a third one. "Seems to be all clear now." Satisfied she had removed all the bugs, she stood up.

Across the parking lot was a strange SUV, sporting blacked out windows. "Oh, maybe just a little peek." *That has to belong to Stranger Danger.* She walked across the parking lot, leaving her debugging equipment on the ground by Jade's car.

One hand cupped around her face she peered inside the SUV. The back seats were down and equipment was scattered everywhere. "Impressive equipment."

One hand held the tracking devices and batteries, with the empty hand she tugged on the door handle. It opened. The top half of her body was inside the SUV, drooling over all the equipment. A faint 'click-ick' vibrated through the air. Rikki's eyes enlarged and froze for a split second. She levitated in the air, pushing distance between her and the SUV as fast as possible.

The explosion launched Rikki across the parking lot. Her chin collided with the ground first, she didn't feel the asphalt burn, yet. The ground shook as the intense heat from the explosion hit her face. Her eyes sealed shut from the mascara on her upper and lower eyelashes melting together. With her thumb and finger she pulled her eyelashes apart.

For a moment, the world surrounding her seemed far-flung as she watched the SUV swallowed up in flames. She pushed her body up off the ground and in a fit of rage threw the tracking devices into the flames. *What the hell is happening to my life? Killing people, cars exploding...what next? No, I don't want to know. Mom, help me through this one.* Rikki tossed up a prayer.

Grace ran out the office door, the hair on her arms stood up at the site of Rikki standing by a burning vehicle, clothes filthy, a bloody raw chin, swollen lip and long dark hair going in every direction. *This has to be a delusion. It can't be real!*

"Rikki! Omigod! What have you done?" Grace screamed.

Lexi stood behind Grace mouth gaped open, speechless.

The sound of Grace's voice pulled Rikki out of her bewilderment. The walk across the parking lot seemed like miles. Rikki noticed a man stepping out of an older Cutlass Supreme that had parked in front of the office. Disillusioned instinct took over Rikki as she pulled her gun and charged toward the man. He was roughly shoved against the car with a gun pointed to his head before he could even shut the car door.

"Who are you?" Rikki demanded.

"Don't shoot, don't shoot!" Lexi screamed running toward Rikki and the man. "It's my boyfriend, don't shoot him!"

"Rikki, let go of him!" Grace yelled following Lexi.

"I'm Barry...Lexi's boyfriend!" He yelled at Rikki along with Lexi and Grace.

"Sorry, sorry." Rikki let go of him and holstered her gun. "Everybody inside." She took another look at the burning SUV. Grace retrieved the debugging equipment Rikki had left on the ground.

Jade stepped out of Rikki's office into the lobby to see what all the commotion was about. "What is going on?" She asked as they all piled in the front door.

"Little explosion...meant for Stranger Danger I'm sure." Rikki answered as she locked all seven deadbolts. Her chin began to throb as blood accumulated on the wound and dripped down her neck.

"Lexi, you're not working here," Barry pulled Lexi close and hugged her.

"Grace." Rikki nodded her head toward the equipment room. "Nobody leave." She instructed Jade, Barry and Lexi.

"No, we are out of here." Barry smarted back.

Rikki's eyes narrowed and she approached Barry until she was in his face. "Listen, tough guy, no one is going out that door right now, so you better keep your mouth shut and your tush parked. You don't have a clue what's going on here." She said with clenched teeth.

"I don't have to know what's going on here! All I need to know is Lexi's not working for you! I love her and value her life! You don't!"

"I value every person's life in here, you idiot, that's why I don't want anyone to leave. So, if you don't want to die, sit down and shut-up." Rikki's patience was missing in action.

"Barry, please, just chill out for a minute." Lexi couldn't take anymore she buried her head in his chest.

"See, now you've upset her," Rikki said then walked away with Grace and disappeared into the equipment room.

"What now?" Grace asked.

"Jade is in deeper than she even knows. I'll tell you that right now."

"Maybe she does know that's why she came here and won't leave. I know she's scared to death." Grace threw in her two cents.

"True. I suspect that her purse, clothes something on her person is bugged. We need to strip her down and burn everything...I happen to know where there's *a-tsi-la* (fire)." Rikki dug around looking for some kind of clothes for Jade.

"I've got my workout clothes in my office. She can wear those until we come up with something better." Grace offered.

"Perfect. Will you tell her? My mood sucks right now...no bedside manner at all."

"Hmm...I didn't notice. Do something with your bloody chin." Grace made a disgusting face, spun around on one foot and left the room.

Rikki picked up the phone and dialed Stone. She envisioned him in uniform standing beside his patrol car. A smile swept her face. Bam! The vision in her head switched, he now stood naked in front of her. *Oh gawd, hello, I did not see that coming, hmmm.* She shook her head, like an etch-a-sketch, to erase the nude picture.

"Officer Russell." He answered.

His voice caught her off guard. *You were just u-ya-ti-ga* (naked) *in my head.* "Uh, h-hello." She stuttered a moment, then remembered why she called. "Oh, are you still with Ssst...." She started to say Stranger Danger but decided not to. "Uumm, with that guy?"

"Yip, we're at Urgent Care. He started flippin' out, like shakin' and jerkin'. He's gettin' his nads looked at too. You did a number on this poor guy."

"Nats?" She misunderstood him.

"Gooooo-nads!" Officer Stone Russell exaggerated the word.

Rikki giggled slightly. "I get it! Are you with him right now?"

"Yip. Hey, I heard something about an explosion at your office. I tried to call your cell. What's goin' on there?"

"Ask him if he drives a black SUV and if it was parked at the far end of my parking lot." Rikki ignored his question. She felt the naked vision coming back and shook her head again.

A few seconds later Officer Stone Russell came back to the phone, "he said yes."

"Ask him if his equipment was scattered all over the back."

A few seconds later, "no, nice and tidy."

"Ask him if he left his doors unlocked." *No, no, no...stop being naked in my head!*

A few seconds later, "no, they are locked."

"Ask him if he has good insurance." She focused on her pen going in circles on a sheet of paper. *His beefy thighs...* She bounced her head off a nearby wall.

A few seconds later, "yes."

"Tell him he may be sore right now, but I saved his life by having him arrested."

A few seconds later, "he said, what are you talking about?"

"I looked in his SUV and all the equipment in the back was scattered everywhere. He has some nice stuff by the way...or had...I didn't have the door open for two seconds and I heard this clicking noise. I swear it had to be a motion activated bomb...it was meant to kill him...but instead it knocked me on my head... got a little scrap on my chin and strange visions keep popping in my head. Other than that, no one was injured. What is his name and why is he following Jade?"

"Hold on, I think I need to break this to him gently." Officer Stone Russell had dread in his voice.

Forty-five seconds ticked by and Rikki was tired of holding. "Heeeelllllloooo? I'm hanging up! I'm not a good holder on-er! Stoooone? Are you naked? Can you hear me? I'm hanging up now!"

"Rikki! Shut-up! Give me two more seconds, can you do that?" Stone was getting frustrated with her.

"*Sa-quu* (one), *ta-li* (two)...bye." She counted in Cherokee but didn't hang up.

"Hey!" He thought she was hanging up. "His name is Abner Stickels."

"Oh...well, I'm going to call him Stranger Danger. I'll never remember that name."

"Says he was hired to protect Jade." Stone continued.

"From what? Who hired him?" Rikki started to get excited.

"Hold on." He was getting tired of being in the middle.

"Hello?" It was Stranger Danger, aka, Abner Stickels.

"Hello? Who's this?" Rikki wasn't sure.

"This is Abner Stickels."

A slight giggle got away from Rikki; she really didn't like his name. "Oh, yeah, soooo, who hired you? And what were you protecting Jade from?" Rikki got right to the point.

"Who is this?" He asked, unsure whom he was speaking with.

"Rikki Rankin. I beat you down like a ragdoll earlier. Why did you attack me anyway...never mind it doesn't matter now. Probably a good thing you did or you'd be dead right now."

A grunt filtered across the phone line followed by a thud. "Rikki?" It was Stone again.

"Where'd he go?"

"He doesn't want to talk to you. He basically threw the phone at me."

"Then you need to fill me in.... or tell him I'm on my way there. Which reminds me...can you come and get us? I don't want to drive any cars parked in my lot."

"Gawd, Rikki slow down. You're jumping from one subject to another! Here's what I know. Abner Stickels is a Private Investigator from New York. He won't tell me who hired him. Something to do with a Miles Casteel though...."

"He's dead." Rikki interrupted.

"This Miles guy? Don't answer that...I'm tellin' you what I know, don't interrupt me. He is supposed to be protectin' Jade Brackin. Evidently, Miles was bein' harassed and he worried about Jade bein' harmed because of him. Uh-oh, yeah, he attacked you because he heard you unholster your gun. He thought you were gonna shoot him too...ya know like Greg Hayes. He heard about that." Stone tried to answer all her questions. "Did I cover everything?" He took a deep breath.

"Yes, you did. Now can you come and get us?" *U-ya-ti-ga* (naked) *if possible, no, stop it.* "If not, can you send someone in a marked car to get us?"

"Let me see what I can do. We have some units there already." He was trying to think who he heard respond to the call of an explosion. "Would you call me ever so often just so I know you're all right? This case is dangerous."

"I will." They both hung up. Rikki knew what was in store for her the next couple of days. She made four more phone calls, packed a duffel bag with equipment, and then went to the bathroom to look at her chin.

Grace wrote a note and laid it on the desk, instructing Jade to change clothes and not to say a word. Jade did as she was told without asking questions.

Jade was decked out in Grace's pale pink Nike jogging suit. She stood slightly slouched, oblivious to what was going on around her. She didn't want to know. She'd do what she was told with high hopes all this murder stuff would go away.

Tiny little rich woman. Grace thought. *Hope those pants don't fall off of her at an inopportune moment. Looks like she's been dipped in a bottle of Pepto-Bismol. Gawd is that what I look like when I wear that? I do love the color of Pepto.*

Lexi and her boyfriend, Barry, sat in the lobby not speaking. Lexi showed him around the office, proud of her new place of employment. Barry obviously wasn't as excited.

Rikki's cell phone rang she flipped it open and answered. "*O-si-yo* (hello)?"

"Hey Rikki, I'm at the back door, ready to transport y-all." Officer Hixon informed her. She could tell he had a huge dip tucked between his lip and teeth by the way he talked.

"I'll gather the troops and be out in just a minute. *Wa-do* (thank you)." She hung up.

Grace's office was just down the hall so that was the first stop. There was Jade in her Pepto-Bismol outfit. Grace was putting all Jade's clothes in a bag along with her purse and the blue gym bag that she carried fifty thousand dollars in. Grace swiped the Super Sweep debugging wand over the items and the lights flashed. There was some kind of device somewhere but Grace didn't have time to find it.

"Oh, that's *u-yo-i* (bad)." Rikki whispered and pointed to Jade.

"What?" Jade mouthed.

"Awful." Grace translated Rikki's Cherokee. She only knew from Rikki's expression what it meant.

"That's exactly what I was thinking...in English, of course." Jade whispered back. "Isn't there something we can do about my attire?" She was desperate.

"I did the best I could with such short notice." Grace laughed without sound. "Everything's in the bag that needs to be trashed." She informed Rikki as they walked out.

"Let's just leave it here for now...whoever it is will think she's here. I've got an idea. What size do you wear, Jade?" Rikki pulled out her cell phone and dialed.

"Four or extra small and a five shoe." Jade answered.

Rikki and Grace looked at each other at the same time and both rolled their eyes. They stood five foot seven inches, towering over Jade at least six inches. Their bones wouldn't fit into a size four. The outfit Jade was sporting was a seven, three sizes too big.

Rikki flipped open her cell phone and dialed. "Kam, it's Rikki. Remember those britches I said were cute? Do you have those in a four?"

"Hey, Rikki. Yes, we have a four." Kam answered.

"Will you get a pair of those ready? If you'd pick out an extra small shirt to match that would be great and a pair of shoes in a five...comfortable ones, not heels."

"Sure. Hey, did you hear that explosion?" Kam asked.

"Boy did I! The upper half of my body was in the SUV that exploded!"

"Omigod! I'll bag everything up and have someone bring it to your car. You don't need to come in." Kam seriously didn't want Rikki in her store.

"That hurts my feelings. We'll be in a police car. Will five hundred cover it?"

"Are you being arrested?" Kam didn't know what to think about her business neighbor.

"No, I'm the good guy, remember? What about the five hundred?" Rikki's chin was getting tight, and she was starting to feel the sting.

"Yes it should, if not, we'll settle up later."

"*Wa-do* (thank you), Kammy," Rikki hung up. She looked at Jade. "Feel better now that you will have clothes to fit?"

"Yes, thank you." Jade was grateful. She didn't know she would be wearing rock star clothes from Los Angeles.

Grace informed Lexi and Barry that they were ready to go. Rikki loaded her briefcase with the fifty thousand dollars and a file that she had started on Jade Brackin.

"Shotgun!" Rikki secured her spot in the front seat of the patrol car.

Everyone loaded up in the backseat of the patrol car while Rikki lingered behind and installed extra security measures at the office. She sent out a text to everyone in her address book that read: DO NOT DARKEN THE DOORWAY OF MY OFFICE UNTIL FURTHER NOTICE.

She threw a magnetic sign on the metal door that read: DO NOT ENTER – SMITH & WESSON SECURITY SYSTEM. It wasn't a joke.

Rikki jumped into the front seat of the patrol car. "No one come back here until you hear from me or Grace. It could mean life or death." She couldn't be more serious.

7

JADE WAS INSTRUCTED TO change clothes in the backseat of the patrol car while everyone looked the other direction. She didn't want to but she did after discarding the high-dollar price tags. "I didn't know clothes of this style were so expensive." She mentioned quietly.

"We might be hillbillies, but we know how to dress like a rock star. You don't have to be in New York to buy high-dollar clothes." Grace said letting her in on the secret.

"I didn't mean it like that. I don't think you're hillbillies." Jade was embarrassed. She pulled a pair of boots out of the bag. "This is ludicrous!"

Grace giggled. The tag on the boots read: *Love Hurts Rain Boot in Purple*

They were two shades of purple, flames running upwards decorated with guns and red roses. A price tag of sixty dollars.

"I guess it's better than the alternative." Jade tried to be polite.

"What is going on back there?" Rikki twisted in her seat and spotted the boots. "Omigod! I love, love, love those! Too frickin' cute!"

"I like them too." Grace confessed. "The look on Jade's face was priceless!"

"We will get us a matching pair...want too?" Rikki asked Grace.

"I sure do!"

Jade reluctantly slide the loud purple rocker rubber boots onto her feet and sighed.

"Hey, let's play scrabble!" Rikki said to Officer Hixon.

"I was thinking the same thing. It's been a long time. Start making calls," Officer Hixon said reaching for his cell phone in his shirt pocket. "Thhpp, thhpp." He spit out sunflower seed shells into a paper cup.

"Gross! What's spewing out of your mouth?" Rikki snarled her upper lip.

Officer Hixon laughed. "Perv...it just shells." He revealed the new sunflower seeds in his mouth as he stuck his tongue out.

"I wasn't being a perv...you were just like Thhpp, Thhpp... didn't know what was up."

"I love scrabble! When are we gonna play?" Grace was excited.

"Not that kinda scrabble, Grace." Rikki and Officer Hixon said in harmony.

Lexi and Barry were silent in the backseat. Mostly, out of fear, they didn't know what was going on or where they were going. Lexi was doing a bang up job of rolling with it. Jade felt like she was having an out-of-body experience. Dressed like a rock star with total strangers who she deemed bizarre, she suffered from culture shock at the very least.

"What kinda scrabble is it? Is it painful?" Lexi asked.

Officer Hixon and Rikki busted up laughing. "*Thla* (no)...it doesn't hurt! It's designed to cause confusion to anyone trying to tail us." Rikki explained. "Just remain calm and get down when Officer Hixon tells us too."

Officer Hixon turned left to the on-ramp from 91st Street and went north on Highway 169. He knew they were being tailed by a white SUV but didn't divulge that to anyone. Nearing the 81st Street exit, Officer Hixon glanced in his rearview mirror and caught a glimpse of two patrol cars closing in on them. "Get ready for the action, y-all." He paused to allow the patrol cars to get closer, "Get down now!" Rikki, Grace, Lexi, Barry and Jade all slide down in the seat.

They passed 81st Street exit, as one of the patrol cars flew by them, the other patrol car slid in behind them. Another patrol car jumped on the highway at 81st Street and passed two of the other patrol cars then slid in the line. The four cars played leapfrog, making it impossible for anyone to distinguish between the patrol cars. At 71st Street another car joined the convoy, passing three patrol cars and sliding into line.

"What is going on?" Grace so bad wanted to rise up to take a peek.

"Right now there's five patrol cars...no, make that six...we're playing leapfrog. We're at the 41st Street exit, there's another one...we now have seven cars all jumbled up on Highway 169. Three more miles and we all flip on the lights and take different exits." Officer Hixon explained the game of scrabble that he, Rikki and Officer Stone Russell invented several years ago, during another investigation of Rikki's.

"Rikki, how many times have you done this?" Grace asked.

"I don't know, several times through the years. I would love to be a car passing by and see it all happen but I'm always in the floorboard." She laughed.

"I have never heard of anything like this in my life. I don't know if I should be scared or feel safe." The confusion in Jade's voice was apparent.

"I hate to admit it but I feel pretty safe right now." Barry said.

"I love every minute of this! And I'm getting paid." Lexi said.

Officer Hixon weaved in and out of the other six patrol cars, another patrol car would weave in and out then they'd slide back into line. "It's time for lights and then the big finish." He flipped the lights on, as did all the other patrol cars.

"I'm sure we've lost any and all tails at this point," Officer Hixon studied his rearview mirror, no visual of the tail. He raised his sunglasses to the top of his head as all the cars increased their speed.

"I'm sensing we are close to I-244." Rikki was tired of being in the floor.

"We are." Officer Hixon verified.

The first patrol car remained on Highway 169. The second patrol car shot to the right on the Admiral Exit. The first patrol car took the next exit onto I-244 east. Officer Hixon was driving the third car. He took the I-244 exit west. The fourth car went straight, staying on Highway 169. The fifth car jumped off at the Admiral exit, the sixth patrol car veered west on to I-244 and the last car went east on I-244. Within seconds all the patrol cars had scattered in four different directions. If the tail was brave enough to follow the convoy of patrol cars scattering around the highway, he would not have a clue which one to follow at this point in the game and it was just a game.

"All clear, you can get up now." Officer Hixon informed his passengers.

"Good job! Nice piece of drivin'," Rikki cheered and clapped her hands.

"That was fun. I like that kind of scrabble too," Grace clapped with Rikki.

Jade remained silent and stared out the window. Lexi and Barry sat up in the seat and watched Rikki and Grace clap with excitement. Lexi wished Barry wasn't there so she could clap too.

"You know where you're taking us now?" Rikki asked Officer Hixon.

"Sure do. We took the long way around but our ETA is around twenty minutes."

"Where are we going?" Barry asked.

"You'll see when we get there. We have to take every precaution." Rikki was vague. "You and Lexi won't have to stay. Officer Hixon will take you home. Just don't get your car until it's been checked for bombs."

Lexi looked at Barry. That would sound far-fetched, even dangerous to Barry had he not been there. Lexi waited for him to pitch a fit. He didn't. As it were, he totally understood and knew that Rikki and Grace would do anything to protect those around them. He was calm, almost even pleasant. Lexi smirked.

Officer Hixon pulled into the *Marriott Hotel* on 71st and Lewis, parked in front of the doors and let Rikki, Grace and Jade out of the car, and then quickly drove away. Rikki led the way, slightly in front of Jade and to the right. Grace walked directly behind Jade, smirking the entire time at Jade's newfound rockism style. Through the doors and to the right were the elevators. One glimpse toward the elevators revealed a group of intoxicated people, so Rikki redirected them up the plush stairs that were positioned in front of the main doors, to the second floor. She pushed the up button four times in a row, stepped back and looked at the lights above the doors. Grace stepped up to the buttons and pushed the up button four times in a row, stepped back and watched the lights above the elevators.

"That's not going to make it come any quicker." Jade announced.

"Yes, but it makes us feel like we are doing something to push it along." Rikki said, looking over Jade to scan the area behind them. Rikki felt like a sitting duck at a target range. She wanted to get Jade out of the public eye immediately before someone recognized any of them. She couldn't help but grin when she looked back at Jade. *Bet she never thought she'd wear such an outfit!* Giggle.

"Useful...gotta feel useful." Grace said not taking her eyes off the elevator lights.

So far so good, no one knows we're here. Rikki's eyes darted around the second floor. *Ding,* the elevator stopped. All three of them waited impatiently for the doors to part. They slid open, exposing the same intoxicated people that were downstairs.

"Seriously?" Rikki murmured.

"Come on in! We'll make room." One of them yelled.

Rikki and Grace looked at each other and shrugged. On a normal day they wouldn't even entertain the thought of crawling into an elevator so full. They squeezed in the elevator with Jade between them. The rest of the elevator patrons were enjoying every minute of the crowded ride, hooting and hollering as if they were still at the hotel club.

"What floor, ladies?" Someone yelled.

"Eight." Rikki answered.

"That's where were going." Someone else blurted.

"Oh great." Jade whispered.

"Damn." Rikki rolled her eyes.

"Peachy, just peachy," Grace faked a smile. *At least no one has recognized us.*

"Rikki, how do you know we're on the eighth floor? We didn't check in." Jade asked.

"Our bodyguard checked us in and is securing the room as we speak. He text messaged me the info." Rikki informed her.

"Oh wow, a bodyguard. I'm glad to know you are taking this so seriously." Jade was impressed that Rikki had already arranged everything. *She may be absurd but she does know what she's doing. I shouldn't judge I'm bizarre acting as well at this juncture in my life.*

"Of course I am. Have you noticed my chin? How about my lip? Anytime I get injuries that requires ointment...it's serious," Rikki watched the floors pass by way of numbers.

"I want out of this vator." Grace was about to hyperventilate.

"You and me both." They hated crowds. Floor six flashed. "Not much longer."

By the time they reached the eighth floor Jade's ears were ringing from the noise level inside the elevator. "I'm in hell." She said to no one in particular.

"Yes, but you look like a rock star." Grace teased.

"If you're gonna be in hell, might as well look good doin' it." Rikki joked. "Nice boots by the way...love love love them! Never know might be your country club friends' new fad."

On the eighth floor the elevator came to a complete stop. The door slid open. Jade gasped and tried to step back further into the hell of the elevator but couldn't. Rikki and Grace grabbed Jade by the arms as she nearly fainted. The roar from the elevator was deafening. Rikki and Grace held tightly to Jade as they roared with laughter along with the fifteen or so drunks.

Five feet from the elevator doors a man crouched, pants down around his ankles and his bare ass aimed at the crowded elevator. Apparently, Jade had never been mooned at such close range, if at all. The bare-assed man looked around his shoulder with a proud smile at his audience. When his attention focused on Jade, a frightened stranger, and the shock on his face made the whole situation all the more funny.

"Herman!" Grace yelled at the bare-assed man.

"Why am I not surprised?" Rikki said as she pushed Jade out of the elevator. "Jade, that ass has been in my hair." Rikki pointed to Herman's bare white ass then gave it a stern slap.

Jade's eyes popped out of her head. "You know this man?" Jade's cultural shock had reached a new level. "I don't want to know how his bum got in your hair."

"Grace? Crazy Cora?" Herman was surprised to see them, obviously. He grabbed at his pants that drooped around his ankles. He called Rikki Crazy Cora from the movie *Quigley Down Under*. In turn, Rikki called him, Roy.

"Herman! You're such an idiot!" Herman's wife Janet laughed as she elegantly pulled her long strawberry blond hair behind her shoulders. She tried to salvage a grain of dignity despite her husband's actions.

The group unloaded from the elevator and congregated in the hallway. Rikki became unnerved and tried to get through the crowd unnoticed, dragging Jade and Grace along with her.

"I didn't think anyone else would be on the elevator..." Herman started to explain.

"Why do you think your elevator beat ours? Because we stopped to pick-up more people!" Janet still laughed.

"What are you doing here? We saw you guys on the news."
Herman blew their cover.

"I've been meaning to call," Janet paused, "Your face looks
awful."

"It's alright, nothin' that won't heal. I'll..." Rikki was cut
short.

"Everybody get against the wall with your hands on your
head!" Johnny, the bodyguard, yelled. His arms were extended
toward the crowd with a .45 Semi-automatic Ruger clutched
in his hands. He jerked the gun to the right, then to the left as
he tried to see everyone at once. Johnny was six foot tall, two
hundred thirty pounds of pure muscle, dark hair and blue eyes,
and highly trained to take control of a chaotic situation.

"Johnny, it's okay! We know most of these people!" Grace
charged toward Johnny with her hands in front of her, fingers
spread wide. "Its okay, its okay!"

Every drop of blood drained from Jade's face, she was white
as snow and froze in time. Rikki scooped her up beneath one
arm and followed Grace. The intoxicated group fell silent and
complied with Johnny's request.

Johnny shoved his gun into a holster that hung on his belt
next to a gold shield badge. "Thought you were in danger." He
said.

"We need to change locations." Rikki said to Johnny.

"Yes, we do. I'll make the arrangements," Johnny motioned
for the three girls to start walking down the hall.

"Hey Roy! We all saw your balls!" Rikki yelled.

"Did ya like it, Crazy Cora?" Herman yelled back.

Rikki snarled her upper lip, "you ain't right!"

"Well, that's a fine how do-ya-do!" Grace chuckled.

Johnny secured the stairwell and guided Rikki, Grace and
Jade to the ground floor.

8

JOHNNY DROVE HIS PRECIOUS cargo to another location. He wasn't properly introduced to Jade, but he knew she was his mission for the next few days. He would not waiver that position.

"Johnny, please, get us somewhere we can relax. I'm exhausted." Grace was tired of all the explosive drama.

"I'll second that." Jade agreed.

"Hang tough girls."

Rikki sat in the front seat of his tan Tahoe, staring out the window. *I need to read the police report on Miles Casteel's murder. I should go look at the corpse too. Yuk. His will, need to find out when it's gonna be read. First, I will talk to Jade one more time...tell her I know she's lying. Man, I gotta lot to do.* She closed her eyes. *A-yo* (ouch)! *My chin and lip do not hurt. Mind over matter.*

Johnny pulled into the Cherokee Casino and Resort just east of Tulsa. He handed the valet attendant the keys then opened the back door to let Jade and Grace out.

Johnny lugged Rikki's duffle bag and checked-in at the front desk. Rikki, Grace and Jade stood with their necks bent backwards under the five-foot, glass chandelier and admired it.

"That's really pretty." Grace said.

"Yes, it is." Jade agreed.

"The Cherokees sure know how to party," Grace looked around the Casino.

"Yes, they do." Jade agreed, again.

"Ahh, look at the snakes, they're smiling." Grace said about the snakes painted under the five-foot glass chandelier.

"They're not smiling, Grace, they're grrrrr'ing." Rikki showed her teeth to demonstrate what the snakes were actually doing.

"Oh. Or that."

"I'd rather think they were smiling." Jade liked Grace's interpretation better.

"Geez...you two are so girly! But I am glad to see you're bonding." Rikki spun around to see what Johnny was doing.

Her eyes met Rocky Payne's, a six foot four inch tall drink of water, light brown hair, green eyes, and a captivating smile. *I'm thirsty.* He was Rikki's weak spot. Their on-again, off- again relationship made her crazy, although it was mostly her fault. Even when they were off again, they were on, each felt the same way but neither would say it out loud. This had been going on for over a year. There stood the six foot four inch reason Jaxon Drywater doesn't have a chance with her.

Their eyes locked, neither said a word. The briefcase stuffed with fifty thousand dollars in her right hand suddenly became cumbersome.

There's my safe place to fall. He was wearing a black suit with a red shirt and tie. He called it a Zoot Suit. He hated it, but the casino required him to wear it in the blackjack pit. He looked incredibly handsome but Rikki preferred him in his cowboy boots, Wranglers and hat. When he wasn't working he was roping in rodeos, going to the stockyards, feeding the cattle, building fences, normal cowboy stuff. Rikki loved that about him. Good ol' country boy.

"Hey, Rikki..." Grace turned around, "...oh no, this can't be good." She discovered them locked in a gaze.

Rocky started to speak. Rikki shook her head and looked away. Rocky knew her well enough to know now was not the time, for whatever reason. Just by looking, he also knew she was involved in an intense investigation. The wild look in her eyes bothered him the most. Her clothes although nice, were bloody, not that unusual for Rikki. Her face scrapped, swollen and bloody, again, not that unusual for Rikki. He wanted to know what was going on. He wanted to help and he wanted to hold her, but instead he walked away.

"Rikki, let's go." Grace nudged her.

"We're all checked-in, right this way." Johnny motioned for them to lead the way.

With a heavy heart Rikki watched her cowboy walk away. He walked down the stairs to the gaming floor and looked over his shoulder. A sweet smile crossed his lips. He was surprised to see her still standing on top of the steps, watching him. Rikki pressed her lips together, causing her right cheek to expose a deep dimple then she strolled off toward Johnny.

"What was all that back there?" Jade asked Grace.

"Well, that was Rocky..." Grace started to tell their history.

"Shut-up." Rikki didn't want to hear it.

"I will not." They entered the elevator. "So anyway, they've dated for over a year. But Rikki got it in her head that she couldn't trust him. I'm not sure why, really...so she told him they shouldn't see each other anymore. That lasted, I don't know, a couple weeks maybe. They got back together and she did the same thing again, twelve times." Grace rolled her eyes.

"Guess I'm caught up on Rikki's love life." Johnny smirked.

"Not really. But in the end...she's still alone." Grace clarified.

Rikki was silent. *Once a playboy always a playboy...he just wasn't that into me. Not much of an effort on his part. Or mine. Who cares, I need a man for one thing and any stranger will do. That's not true...I don't do strangers...sounded good though. I should say it out loud. Naw, let 'em talk about me like I'm not here, she's just tryin' to get me to talk about Rocky and I won't do it. Is it possible that I, I, llll...llll...vvvv...damn...care for him? Shake it off...* Rikki quivered, not good enough, she shook her head rapidly for half a second. *Better. I need counseling. I won't get it, but I do need it.*

"We're in room six twenty six." Johnny said when the elevator stopped on the sixth floor. "And six twenty four. We have adjoining rooms." They meandered down the hall with an eye on the room numbers.

Wonder what Rocky's been up too? I need him right now. No I don't. It would be nice to have him right now...that's what I meant. Push it out of my head. Murder. Murder. Murder...who committed the murder? Rikki wandered into the hotel room, startled by her reflection in the mirror. *Omigod! I need to change clothes... no wonder people were looking at me funny. I have no clothes with me...dammit! I don't feel like talking to anyone right now.* She sat down on the edge of king-sized bed and fell back.

"This is nice." Grace said. "I love the Indian artwork." She and Jade were in the adjoining room with two queen-sized beds. Red earth tones covered the walls with a Native American border. Bedding with red, tan and brown earth tones blended with the cozy decor.

"It is quaint." Jade replied. She opened the big wooden doors on the entertainment center and exposed the TV. "Dare we turn it on?"

"I'm sure there will be something about the explosion on the news tonight. Rikki hasn't said one word since she saw Rocky. Well, except shut-up. Where is she?" Grace wondered into the other room and found Rikki passed out on the bed, with her legs hanging off the side. "Guess she's had a rough day." She shut the door between the rooms so they wouldn't disturb her power nap.

Johnny pulled a chair closer to the door and sat down. He was on full alert, the only difference between him and a Rottweiler guard dog—he walked on two legs and carried a gun.

Grace and Jade ordered room service. When it finally arrived, the knock on the door had Johnny in an attack stance with his gun aimed at the door. He looked through the peephole, opened the door and said, "I'll take it from here." He rolled the cart inside the room. "Go on, get outta here." Without shilly-shallying the service man took off down the hall. He didn't want any part of Johnny.

"You didn't tip him! You have to tip him!" Jade was appalled. She jumped up off the bed and ran to the door.

Johnny stopped her. "You're not going out there."

"Then you must summon him back here. Hurry, before he reaches the elevator."

"You're not kidding. Can't believe I'm doing this." He opened the door and stepped out into the hall. "Hey, mister! Could you come here a minute."

The service man reluctantly returned to Johnny. Jade handed Johnny twenty dollars. "Do you want change?" He asked.

"No. That's a standard tip." Jade said.

"Maybe for you. Here ya go, dude." Johnny handed the money to the service man.

"Thank you. Thank you so much sir." He halfway bowed and didn't make eye contact.

"No problem." Johnny shut the door. "Happy?"

"Yes, thank you." Jade had a big heart, but she lacked common sense about safety, Johnny thought.

"Good. Now, don't ever do that again. Don't assume you can walk out this door, because you can't. Not without me...and don't spring shit up on me like that. I was hired to do a job and that's what I'm here to do. I will not let you, Grace or Rikki down. Understood?"

"Ummm, yes...I do appreciate it...I guess." Jade did feel safe and was grateful but it was all-new to her. She would work harder at being a good...*what am I? Captive? Hostage? No, I'm protected...wonder what the ladies at the country club would think of all this?*

Grace watched Jade and Johnny. *They need to bond.* Giggle. *Could they be more opposite? What a comical pair they make.* She dug into her food.

"So Jade, where's your husband?" Grace blurted.

"Overseas on business...it's probably more pleasure, if you ask me."

"Does he know what's going on here? What you're going through?" Grace was astonished by her frank answer.

"No. I can't get in touch with him. I've tried but no answer. Honestly, we aren't that close. He has his life and I have mine. Nothing in particular happened. We just grew apart and haven't pushed to rekindle that loving feeling." Jade answered.

That's nice to know. Can't wait to tell Rikki. "That's too bad." She said.

"What about you, you married?"

"No. I've been seeing a guy, Mike, for five years. We keep that loving feeling right on track." She grinned.

Jade smiled back. "Good for you. And Rikki she just flounders about, alone?"

"Well, yes and no. She's independent, but she's not always alone. She dates. A lot."

"She has a thing for this Rocky, you think?" Jade was genuinely interested.

"Oh, I think all right! She won't admit it, but I've seen her do things that she's never done before. One of them is going back after breaking up, and breaking up again, but still talking to him almost every day in one form or another. Never known her to call a man on the phone—she calls him. Never known her to call a man honey or baby—she does him. Then, there's Jaxon Drywater. I think that's more lust, but she won't even get close enough to find out...won't even talk to him on the phone. I really like Jaxon, he's tried so hard, and he does care for her. I'm not so sure about this Rocky. There's something she's not telling about him, I just know it."

"How intriguing. He is handsome." Jade wanted more gossip.

"Oh yeah...he's typical of what she usually goes for...not falls for though. Tall, handsome...he's not intimidated by her, like most men are. That may be her fascination with him." Grace yawned. "It's funny, he gives her crap and surprisingly she takes it...not lying down of course, but he can put her in her place. Never seen anything like it."

"Just from the few hours I've spent with Rikki...I'd love to see someone be able to put her in her place. I don't mean that in an ugly way, please understand. She's just sooo...." Jade couldn't think of the word.

"I know what you mean."

"I've never met anyone like her. I'm sure she's different under different circumstances, but right now she can be downright scary." Jade tucked her bleach blonde hair behind her ears.

Johnny smirked at the conversation. He knew exactly what they were talking about.

Grace finished her meal and stacked the dishes on the cart. "It's been over an hour, I'm gonna check on Rikki." She moved across the room to the adjoining door.

For her own safety she quietly opened the door, with no sudden movements. A startled Rikki, out of a sound sleep, equaled a gun in your face before her eyes were all the way open. Two steps in and Grace jerked to a stop. Lying on the floor were Rikki's bloody clothes and a black suit—the Zoot Suit. Her holster and gun placed on the nightstand. Grace backed out of the room and carefully shut the door.

"Well, she's fine. Rocky's putting her in her place, all right... rekindling that loving feeling. They're in there spooning, sound asleep." Grace announced.

"What?" Johnny's blood boiled, he didn't even hear him enter the room.

"What is spooning?" Jade asked halfway frightened of the answer.

"They're lying like spoons in a drawer...snuggling." Grace explained.

Jade laughed with excitement. "That is marvelous! Whew! I can't believe it."

"Oh, I can. If they had sex...I'm gonna be pissed! I could be home with Mike right now." Grace grumbled.

Rocky had cradled Rikki tight while she enlightened him, in a whisper, of the events that had transpired the last few days. His heart broke for her. He let two days go by without calling or texting, he never did that, and now he carried the guilt. She didn't call him either though, why should he feel guilty. *If only I'd turned on the TV. Between work, the cattle and horses, I just didn't have time to watch TV.* Rikki cried herself to sleep in his arms. Not a bellowing cry, a silent watery-eyed cry. *I'm here now. That's all that matters.*

He had been Rikki's soft place to fall for over a year. Seen her vulnerable, a side she doesn't show anyone. Rikki acknowledged that for some absurd reason he elevated every emotion in her. This made the second time he'd seen her cry. Grace had witnessed that maybe once in twenty some odd years.

Rocky rolled over on his back and pulled Rikki to his chest.

She nuzzled in and licked her lips, still half asleep. An unidentified object pressed against her lips, she stuck her tongue out again. "Your nipple fell in my mouth." She said sleepily. The vibration of his deep laugh tickled her ear. *I love his laugh,* was her last thought before she sunk into unconsciousness.

9

THREE AM, RIKKI'S EYES sprung open and her mind reeled so
fast she could scarcely maintain herself. Rocky still had a death
grip on her. She had to get up. Gently, she tried to move his arm
without disturbing him. The palm of his hand alone was bigger
than her entire hand. The stout six-four frame wouldn't budge.
She seemed weak and couldn't quite figure out why.

"Where ya goin', babe?" His grip tightened.

"I gotta get up. Take a shower...get movin' on this murder
thing." She still tried to get up. "Omigod! I'm sore! Every muscle in
my body is screaming right now." She fell across Rocky's chest.

They lay in silence for several minutes. Rikki's body was limp,
in a trance with the rhythm of each breath Rocky inhaled. Even
his smell was relaxing. *Guess I don't have to go this very minute.
Just enjoy the moment.* She squeezed her eyes shut and enjoyed
the feel of his skin, his scent and the bass tone of his voice.

"I'm sorry, honey. Probably from bein' blown through the air
and bouncin' off the ground, on your face," he hugged her. "Gotta
little hitch in your git-a-long."

Is he giggling? He is I'm sure of it. "Why the hell are you
laughing?"

A moment of silence then a deep laugh, short, but still a laugh.
"Did you hear what I said? Blowin' through the air, bouncin' off
the ground...it's just funny.... it is, it is. Who does that?"

"I do, smart ass. And I shot a man...dead...two days ago... three days...I don't' even know what day it is. " The moment was gone, lost forever. Back to the sparring they were so good at.

"A hot shower will help. Then I have to put on bloody clothes. If Stone's on duty, I'm gonna see if he'll come get me and take me home. I have so much to do." She tried to get up again. "Wow, this sucks." Rocky pushed her up. "Thanks. Now can you carry me to the shower, turn on the hot water and throw me in?" She shuffled across the floor barely able to force the steps. It was that painful.

"I'll take you home or wherever you need to go." Rocky sincerely offered.

"Really?"

"Well, yeah." Aggravated she sounded surprised at the offer.

"*Wa-do* (thank you), Rocky."

At three-twenty, Rikki was out of the shower, feeling more alive. Her chin was raw and in need of ointment, lip still swollen, but her muscles had loosened a tad. Still sore—yet better. Due to lack of a brush she scrunched her long hair, in other words, a controlled mess. She yanked bloody clothes onto her clean body. "How do you break into a hotel room?" She asked Rocky. "I mean with the electronic keys and all." She reached toward the nightstand and grabbed her holster, snapped it in place and shoved her pistol inside.

Rocky watched her in amazement. A few hours ago she had a complete melt down in his arms. Now, the real Rikki had emerged. "I'm sure there's a master key...wouldn't you think?" Rocky pondered the question. "I could ask at the desk if I know who's covering it this morning. Why do you ask, sweetie?"

"Because I'm gonna get Jade up ask her a few questions, then I'm gonna break into the crime scene. It's at the Downtown Hotel." She pulled on her cowboy boots and folded her socks over the top of them – kept her socks in place. A sock falling down while chasing a bad guy is a huge pet peeve.

"I did ask." He rubbed his forehead. "Let me guess, I'm your ride?"

"You got it Cowboy," a slight smile crossed her lips. A full-fledged smile would be painful, until she gets that ointment.

"Let me see what I can find out at the front desk" he shook his head, "I'm thinkin' you're gonna owe me big for this."

"Honey, I'll gladly be indebted to you." She flirted.

"Be careful what ya wish for," he pulled her head back gently by the hair, kissed her softly and slipped out the door.

Rikki opened the adjoining door. They were all asleep. Poor Johnny, still positioned in the chair by the door, his head bent back against the wall. *Damn, they had room service.* She maneuvered past the tray, without a sound. Each movement was calculated so not to disturb even the air, a ghost in the night.

Next to Jade's ear she whispered. "Jade, wake up." Her lips touched Jade's ear. "Jade, wake up. Sshh, don't make a sound."

Jade stirred. "It's Rikki I need to talk to you for just a second. Come on follow me."

Jade sat up. Rikki put her finger to her swollen lip and led the way to the other room. Jade still wore the rocker outfit.

"What time is it?" Jade whispered, after Rikki shut the door.

"Around three-thirty. The hour of truth, no more bull crap Jade." They sat at the round table in the corner of the room. Rikki pushed everything on the table back to make room for her notepad.

Jade was silent. *Three-thirty in the morning and she wants to ask questions. Looks like she's already taken a shower. This makes me feel guilty.*

"When's the last time you saw Miles Casteel?" Rikki whispered.

"The day before he was murdered." Jade felt her face flush she realized Rikki knew she had lied earlier. *I will tell her whatever she wants to know this time.*

"Where?"

"Here in Tulsa at the hotel, room number seven twenty-one."

"Were you having an affair?"

"Yes, have been for seven years...or so."

"Does your husband suspect anything?"

"I don't know. He's always away on business, out of the country."

"Would he have you followed?"

"I don't think so, but I can't be sure. We rarely see one another when he is in the country, when we do we barely speak. Honestly, I don't think he cares what I do. It's more a marriage of convenience."

"What's convenient about that? Sounds more like a nuisance to me."

"It all boils down to money. There's too much involved in getting a divorce so we live our separate lives and stay married. It's never been a problem."

"Your lover's dead...I see a problem." Rikki regretted saying that the second it hit air. "Sorry, I didn't mean to sound unsympathetic."

"I guess it's true." Jade's head was heavy.

"Is there anything at all you can tell me that might give me some direction?"

"The first person I thought of when I heard what happened was my sister. I wouldn't put anything past her. She's always conniving."

"As far as she knows she's inheriting millions, right?"

"That's right," Jade yawned.

Rikki's cell phone vibrated, a text message from Rocky: *I'm at the door*

She left Jade sitting at the table wondering where she was going. She opened the door and Rocky walked in waving a card.

"They said this might work." He handed it to Rikki.

"Jade this is Rocky Payne, Rocky this is Jade." Rikki introduced them.

"Nice to meet you." Jade tried to be cordial through her sleepiness.

"You too." Rocky nodded his head.

"Jade go back to bed. I'm gonna run some errands. Thanks for being honest." Rikki opened her briefcase.

"Thank you for everything you've already done for me." Jade meant that. *What errands could you possibly be running at this hour? I probably don't want to know.*

"Just doin' my job. No thanks needed." She removed the copy of the will.

After Jade left the room and shut the door, Rikki placed the will and the money in the built-in safe under the coffee bar. Duffel bag in hand she was ready to go.

"Where to first?" Rocky asked as they entered the elevator.

"Take me home, Daddy."

Rocky drove to Rikki's house, with a detour through Whataburger. It was a two-story house in South Tulsa, with too many neighbors too close together. Rikki preferred to be in the country but for her kids sake she stayed in town. Once inside Rikki wasted no time changing clothes and strapping two more weapons onto her person. She dug in the medicine cabinet for ointment, what a relief, the stinging and tightness vanished. To make her feel more like a girl, she slapped on a little mascara and voila she's ready to perform an illegal B&E.

10

TULSA STREETS WERE DESERTED just before five in the morning. Seventeen silent minutes in Rocky's diesel truck and they arrived at the hotel. Rikki leaped out of the truck and filled her lungs with the crisp October morning air. She noticed Rocky did the same. The effects of an adrenaline rush began to fill her veins as she threw an oversized bag containing equipment she anticipated needing over her shoulder.

"You really need to stop wearing your horseshoe ring upside down." Rikki purposely aggravated Rocky.

"I don't. You wear yours upside down." He shot back. An ongoing argument they had from the night they met.

Almost immediately after their first hello, they noticed each wore a diamond studded horseshoe ring on their right ring finger, the rings matched perfectly. He wore his with the opening facing his wrist and she wore hers with the opening facing her fingertips. Neither could convince the other that the ring was upside down, but they never gave up trying.

"I have better luck than you, so I have to be right." She pointed out.

"Whatever." He dismissed her. "At least mines not bent... yours is bent and upside down." He laughed.

"Don't *whatever* me. You're not as funny as you think you are! I have feelings and you're hurting them!"

"Done did *whatever* you." He grinned. "Rikki Rankin has feelings...that's funny."

"Must have somethin' to do with that hitch in my git-a-long." She shot him a flirty glare. "Let's walk in like we own the place. Be deep in conversation and don't make eye contact with anyone. We'll take the elevator to the ninth floor then take the stairs down to the seventh floor. I don't have a clue if they have cameras so we'll have to be quick." Rikki hastily changed the subject to their illegal B&E mission.

"What's this *we* stuff? I ain't goin' in! You're on your own." Rocky was quick to correct her, with his hands placed on his hips.

"What? I need you to be the lookout. It's really not that big a deal."

"Then why do you need a lookout? I'm really not comfortable with this." She hated it when he argued, but respected him for it.

"Come on...it'll be fun. I'll owe you big time," she looked up through her eyelashes and managed a full-fledged smile, the ointment worked like magic. "Please?"

"Damn, Rikki. I better not get thrown in jail over this." He couldn't say no. She was his weakness and he had a desire to protect her. She certainly didn't need it but the desire still smoldered inside him.

"I can almost promise you won't, baby," she stepped in front of him on tiptoes, pulled his head down and kissed him.

"Almost?"

"C'mon. It'll be *o-s-da* (fine). I'm actually pretty good at this stuff." Her excitement was contagious. She grabbed his hand and marched in the front door. He didn't resist.

Their boots clomped across the fancy white marble floor. Exotic plants were strategically placed throughout the extravagant hotel lobby. A room so enormous Rocky looked small. First-class hotel obviously built for high society rich snobs. The place was empty. No desk clerks or maintenance workers, should they be concerned?

Rocky's heart danced in his chest and his stress level shot up a hundred percent. Rikki had an adrenaline rush, an extra bounce in her step and couldn't wait to get inside the room. She lived for this! She grasped Rocky's arm and hung on tight.

"This is fun, right?" She looked up at him, "deep conversation, remember? Do you see the elevator?"

He moved his eyes around the lobby then looked back down at her, "it's slightly to the right behind that wall."

"Do you feel tiny in here?" They beelined for the elevator.

He managed a smile. "Never thought about it really."

"You look tiny in here." He was three inches short of being a foot taller than her.

"Honey, I'm not tiny."

On the elevator Rocky let out a sigh. "This is nerve racking."

Rikki nonchalantly looked for cameras, none detected. "Naw, it makes you feel alive. I wanna look around the ninth floor...see if there's any cameras. That way we'll know if there are cameras on the seventh floor. Can you move quickly and be invisible? Like *a-do-nv-do* (spirit)?"

"You're kidding, right?"

"Not really. Wonder if anyone's staying on the seventh floor..." Rikki was antsy, tons of questions on her mind. She'd know soon enough. The elevator stopped on the ninth floor.

Rikki was out and searching the hallways before the doors opened all the way. Rocky wasn't as eager. He stayed by the elevator doors until Rikki was satisfied with the search.

"I don't see anything that would indicate even hidden cameras. There's gotta be though. Oh well, let's go for it...*hi-hv-na* (move it)." She opened the stairwell door. Rocky followed against his better judgment.

Rikki flew down two flights of stairs. Her boots barely touched each step. Rocky skipped two steps at a time. They grabbed a breath at the seventh floor door before Rikki clutched the handle and pulled. It was locked.

"What now?" Rocky was relieved the mission couldn't possibly continue.

Short-lived relief, Rikki had a Kwick Pick Gun in the keyhole and the door open in seconds. "That. Follow me." She inched with a smooth shuffle, flat against the wall, to the main hallway. Rocky followed suit not quite as smoothly, still not bad for a tall man with his nerves stuck in his throat. She pulled out rubber gloves and offered Rocky a pair. His were way too small and wouldn't begin to fit over his fingers. He shoved them in his pocket and vowed to himself not to touch anything.

The hallways were clear. They shifted left to room seven twenty-one, each on either side of the door. She shot Rocky a look with wide eyes. The door was cracked about three inches. No movement, no sound. Rikki stretched to see in as far as she could inside the crack. She motioned with one hand for Rocky to stay put. He nodded. She removed her pistol and pushed the door gently and eased inside.

I'm gonna die. Why did I agree to this? I hope she knows what she's doing. What was that noise? Nothing. I think. He took a deep breath.

Rikki went to work with her digital camera, getting pictures of the crime scene as fast as she could. *Looks like Miles struggled.* An expensive lamp on the floor was shattered. Chairs knocked over. Bedding strung across the floor. A huge hole bashed in the wall, drops of blood in the bathroom and several places around the room. Then of course, the stain on the carpet where Miles bled out and died. *Talk to me room...what went on here.* She stood perfectly still, smelling, seeing, feeling, hearing and studying. *Who did this?* She opened the nightstand drawers, Bible in the top drawer, nothing in the bottom drawer. She pushed the bottom drawer back into place but it caught on something. One tug and the drawer fell out. *Damn, just a paper coffee cup.* Now facing the opposite wall she studied the room from a different angle. *Where's the safe? Shouldn't there be a safe in such a fancy room?* She floated across the room to the television and entertainment center. *Something is wrong...what the hell is it?* A canvas painting to the right of the entertainment center and above a desk was cockeyed. *That's it...the smeared gi-ga* (blood) *under the painting...*

*Why is it there? Miles was reaching for something, or stumbled...
he would've landed on the desk...it's possible...* She removed the
painting, turned it over revealing the wood frame the canvas
stretched across. *Notta.* She replaced the painting on the wall,
cockeyed, like she found it. Something silver caught her eye stuck
between the wall and the desk. She moved the desk and retrieved
the silver object. *A flash drive...hhmmm.* She stuffed it in her
pocket and picked up the edge of the desk to move it back.

The second she lifted the desk—she dropped it and drew
her pistol, extended toward the front of the room. Someone
had ducked into the bathroom. Rikki leaped to the extending
wall off the bathroom, one swift motion had her standing in the
bathroom doorway waving her gun from side to side.

Rocky stepped to the side of the pistol. "What the hell are you
doin'?" His anger clutched in his jaw-line. She thought it was sexy
along with the glare in his green eyes.

"What the hell are you doin'?" She shot back, dropping her
gun to her side.

Why did he think she was sexy? She had just pointed a gun
at him. It wasn't the gun she carried. Maybe it was the controlled
mess of her hair, the excitement in her almost black eyes. The
lack of fear, the gun was sexy, he had to admit. It was her in
general; she was gorgeous and exciting – unpredictable.

"I heard someone down the hall. I was just coming in to warn
you. Ya know, so you could...*tsa-ga-se-s-de-s-di* (watch out)."

Rikki pulled the gun up to her shoulder and darted to the
door. "Sorry. You startled me." She stuck her head out the door,
looked both ways and stepped out into the hall against the wall
to the right. She was gone before he could stop her.

Rocky stood in the doorway of the hotel room and watched
Rikki maneuver through the shadows of the dark hallway. *Gawd
Rikki, why do you have to go after them? We should just get outta
here.*

Rikki approached a room filled with vending and ice
machines. It was pitch black inside the room. She saw a silhouette
of what she thought was a man wearing a baseball cap. *Could be*

the cleaning lady, but why hide in the dark? She squinted trying to let her eyes adjust to the pitch-black room. "Get your hands where I can see 'em and step out." Rikki demanded.

A deafening scream filled the air. A Mexican woman was shoved into Rikki knocking her off balance and backwards a few steps. The woman in a maid uniform was screeching in Spanish, tears glistened on her face. Rikki struggled for balance and shifted her sore body away from the Mexican woman but she couldn't escape her. The woman hovered and never shut-up, terror filled her eyes.

The man in the baseball cap bolted out of the room to the left. He ran with the swiftness of a cheetah down the hall to the service elevator. Rikki figured he was five foot eleven inches weighing around one hundred seventy pounds. Short hair, in fact, she couldn't even get his hair color it was so short.

Rocky charged toward Rikki when he heard the lady scream. He knew Rikki was often bruised, scraped, cut, always some kind of injury but he'd never witnessed the action. He didn't like it. His heart dropped when he saw Rikki stumble backward. Lord, how would he have felt if he'd seen her flying through the air and landing on her face, or fighting a full-grown man? *I'm never going on another investigation with her again.* He swore to himself.

"*To-hi-tsu* (how are you)?" He shouted at Rikki.

"*O-s-da* (fine)...get him!" Rikki shouted back.

Rocky didn't think about what he was doing, guided by anger he ran down the hall after the man with a stride that was elongated and impressively rapid. Rikki did the 'stay' hand motion to the Mexican lady and ran behind Rocky. When she reached him in front of the service elevators he was turning circles searching for the man. He was gone.

"Mother humper! That was probably the break I needed to solve this murder!" She kicked at the air.

"Sorry, baby, I tried to catch him. He was more than halfway down the hall before I even saw him." Rocky wished he had caught the man.

"You don't need to be sorry! It's not your fault. As a matter of fact I can't believe you got so involved. You don't even have a *ga-lo* (gun) on you." Rikki smiled at him.

"What the hell was I suppose to do? Watch some dude *a-sa-nu-da-i* (wound) you? Don't ask me to come with you again, Rikki." His voice was gruff and firm. She liked it.

Rikki turned away from him and smiled. She didn't want him to see her smile, "*v-v hi-s-ga-ya* (yes sir)! I'm gonna try and talk to this Mexican woman. Are you going to wait for me in the car...sister?" She still smiled at her smart-aleck remark.

"Shut-up. Don't call me sister." He brushed against her as he tromped down the hall toward the Mexican woman. His strides so extended Rikki had to trot to keep up. She didn't care.

They were able to get the Mexican woman to write down her number and told her they would get back to her with an interpreter. Rikki gave her one hundred dollars to keep quiet about the situation on the seventh floor. She seemed to understand Rikki's charades and hand signals.

"One hundred dollars?" Rocky scolded amazed by the bribe.

"It will be worth it. I'll call Gabriela...she's an interpreter that I trust. I did find, hopefully, a clue in the room. It's a flash drive. Can't wait to see what's on it! Hey, babe?"

"*Wii* (yes)?"

"*Wa-do* (thank you)."

Rocky smiled, shook his head and gazed in her eyes. "No problem, honey."

11

ROCKY DUMPED RIKKI AT the front door of Easy Rent-A-Car. She watched him drive away not knowing when she'd see him again, or if she would. The time they spent together was cherished, but always abruptly over. Never finished. This time she needed him, needed to fall apart and feel safe if only for a moment. She lied to herself about that fact all the way back to the hotel in the Mustang she rented. She didn't need any man.

The electronic key slid into the slot. The buzz of the locks created a racket that had Johnny at the door ready to pounce, which Rikki expected. She stood to the side of the door and pushed it open. No Johnny. She entered the room and the door floated shut. Johnny appeared from behind the bathroom wall and grabbed Rikki, penning her arms to her sides.

"Knock it off Johnny. I'm too sore to play." She distinguished from the way he grabbed her that he was only playing. The pair practiced moves on one another regularly.

"You think a bad guy is going to care if you're sore or not." He made a point. He felt two weapons on her, one hooked to her belt on the right, another in a shoulder holster under her left arm. She couldn't get to either by the way he held her. He snickered.

Rikki lifted her right foot to her hand plastered at her side, pulled out a small .22 caliber gun and put the barrel on Johnny's leg. "I'll blow a hole in your leg if you don't let go of me." She made her point.

"Good one." Johnny let go.

"Are they friends?" Jade asked Grace.

"Yes, that was nothing. Sometimes they street fight until they draw blood."

"Good heavens! I've never seen anything like it."

Grace laughed.

"Grace, do you have medicine? I'm so sore." Rikki asked.

"Did you have sex last night?"

"No. That's not why I'm sore." Rikki was appalled by the question.

"I know it's not why you're sore. I also know Rocky was in your bed last night."

"The last thing on my mind was sex, dang, Grace! Not everything is about sex."

"Who are you and what have you done with Rikki?" Grace folded her arms and glared.

Rikki laughed. "That was an odd thing to come outta my mouth, huh? I feel like I should apologize for saying such a thing." Rikki noticed Grace had showered and was ready to get on with the day ahead of them. It was only six-thirty.

"There you are I was worried for a minute." She dropped her arms and dug in her purse for naproxen. "Here take these." She cupped three pills in her hand.

Rikki held her hand out for the pills. "I see you're ready to go, shall we?" She threw all three pills in her mouth, entered the adjoining room and unloaded the money and the will from the safe into her briefcase.

"I've been waiting patiently." Grace let her know that she'd been ready for a while.

"You two kids have fun." Rikki said to Johnny and Jade as they left the hotel room.

"How are we going anywhere? We don't have any wheels." Grace usually handled such details. Rikki excelled with details in an investigation but relied on Grace for everything else.

"I rented a car. I parked it by the back of the casino. Are you proud?"

"Wow...shocked is more like it." She wasn't kidding.

They walked through the casino, past the penny machines and the blackjack tables. Surprisingly, the casino was busy this early in the morning. *Whoever came up with the noises the machines make did a good job.* Rikki thought as she listened to the casino racket. *Makes me wanna gamble, win something, throw all my money into a machine and...naw...they ain't gonna get my hard earned dollars.* At the machines in front of Twisters Lounge, Grace pulled out a dollar. She put the bill in one of the machines—it did nothing. She hit the side of it, still nothing.

"It doesn't work." She was disappointed.

"It's a five dollar machine. You might want to add four more dollars to that." Rikki smirked. She leaned against the machine and assessed her surroundings while Grace played. *Guess Grace couldn't resist the temptation of the sound.* Giggle.

Two seconds later, "I feel cheated." Grace was disgusted with her one five-dollar spin.

"Are you ready?" Rikki didn't hide her amusement.

"I'm just not a gambler." Grace concluded.

"Me either. I got a Mustang, you wanna drive?" Rikki handed her the keys. "It hurts to drive...I'm so sore."

"Sure, I'll drive. This carpet reminds me of an Indian blanket." Grace admired the carpet and took the keys. "Where we goin'?"

"To visit Melody at the morgue, gonna view us a dead body." Rikki smiled real nice at Grace, but the mischievous laugh that escaped her was pure evil.

"I hate that evil laugh, witchie-poo! I knew from the minute I heard it was a murder case that we'd end up there. You could've gone before you came back to get me. Where'd you go this morning, anyway?" Grace despised visits to the morgue.

"To the crime scene, found a flash drive. And saw a man in a hat that ran from us. I need to get a hold of Gabriela, the interpreter, to interview a Mexican lady" Rikki filled her in on all the details of her morning. Then they planned the rest of their day on the ride to the morgue.

Grace parked at the back door of the morgue and took her time getting out of the car. Rikki waited, not very patiently, at the front of the car. She paced for a moment and mentally prepared to view the dead Miles Casteel. She felt the Whataburger lying heavy in the pit of her stomach. She would never let on but visits to the morgue rattled her inner being, she hated it. *Just get through this without throwing up.* The car door finally opened and Grace stepped out.

"Omigod, you've got to be kidding me!" Rikki yelled and let out a laugh. "You can't possibly go in there like that!"

"Oh yes I am!" Grace had on a pair of swimming goggles that covered her eyes and nose. The pressure from the goggles on her upper lip made it roll up and her blue eyes looked twice their size. "I can't stand the smell and I don't want dead juice in my eyes."

"You just happen to have those in your purse?" *Not a bad idea, wish I had a pair.*

"I came prepared. I knew you'd do this to me so I stuck 'em in my purse yesterday." It sounded like she was talking through her nose.

"*Tla ya-qua-nv-dv ni-tsa-s-dv-v* (I don't know about you)!" Rikki bellowed in Cherokee.

"I have no idea what you just said and I don't care. Let's get this over with." Grace pushed Rikki in front of her to enter first.

The morgue's metal body drawers and white tile flooring were spotless. Melody pilfered around toward the back until she heard the door open. The white jacket she wore intensified her dark skin and big jet-black hair. She had a little too much energy, which made her head bounce and twist side to side as she talked—fast. Rikki loved her visits with Melody.

"Hello, beautiful!" Melody yelled when she saw Rikki.

"*O-si-yo* (Hello)!" Rikki yelled back. Grace walked directly behind Rikki with a handful of Rikki's shirt because her eyes were closed. "Grace is here too." She informed Melody.

Grace peeked around Rikki, "Hello, Mel!"

"You've just tuned into...I did not see that coming! I love it when you two come and visit...that's hysterical!" Melody pointed at Grace and laughed. It wasn't a secret how Grace felt about the place. "What can I do ya for?"

"We need to see one of your tenants. Miles Casteel." Rikki told her.

"Oh sure, he's right over here," Melody led them through the morgue and pulled out a metal drawer. She unzipped the body bag and exposed Miles Casteel's corpse. "Say hello to one Miles Casteel, ladies." She felt like they needed an introduction. Neither said hello. "He's a quiet man. Sleeps a lot." She added.

Grace let out a heavy sigh. "He's dead, Melody." She had left her sense of humor in the car.

"Are you serious? That's why he never asked for pain medicine when I cut his heart out. Or what was left of it. Would you like to see it?" Melody was wired.

"Oh geeze, Melody, you know the answer to that...no, I don't wanna see it! How long you been up?" Rikki recognized her delirious actions.

"Couple days, I really could use some sleep...but I have dead people coming out of my ears. I do like hanging out with them though, they don't bitch. I've thought about crawling into a drawer for a nap."

Rikki giggled. Grace didn't.

Miles Casteel was a handsome man, even in death with a hole in his chest. Rikki noted the salt and pepper hair on his head and on what was left of his chest. His hands had defensive wounds. *I knew he struggled with the assailant. What else can you tell me Miles? That's a huge hole...large caliber weapon. Jade would not have been able to fire a gun that big.*

"It looks like he was shot point-blank. Was there an angle on the point of entry?" Rikki continued to study the corpse while she asked questions.

"Downward, with a .44 caliber, he wasn't going to walk away from his attacker." Melody answered, fluffing her hair with her fingers.

"The perp was taller than Miles then, and strong enough to handle the kick from a large caliber weapon." Rikki was actually talking to herself.

"I would agree." Melody answered.

"Definitely not executed by a tiny five foot one woman, do you concur?" Rikki just liked to use the word concur when she stood around dead bodies, not sure why.

"I do concur, Detective Rankin." Melody smiled.

"Do you concur, Grace?" Rikki cast a glimpse toward Grace, big mistake.

Grace stood over the human carcass with her eyes closed tight under the goggles. "I concur." She squeezed out. Melody and Rikki's laughter echoed through the morgue. "Y-all really are gonna wake the dead if you don't calm down." Grace scared herself with the thought.

"Rikki, why do you bring her? You know she hates this." Melody was curious.

Rikki still laughed at Grace. "Entertainment. No, I'm just kidding. Grace what have you learned with your eyes closed?" Rikki knew she didn't miss a thing.

"Mr. Casteel was shot with a large caliber weapon from an angle that only someone taller could have administered. He struggled with the perp therefore; it was not our client that committed this heinous crime. If it were her, Mr. Casteel would've stopped her during the struggle. She's just a tiny thing. I did peek a little and saw his hands. Rikki thinks he was somewhat handsome from the tone in her voice. She also knows 'hat man' didn't do it either, and she's wondering who he is and what he was doing at the crime scene. Melody tends to talk out of her ass when she's sleep deprived and that amuses Rikki. And for whatever reason, Rikki loves to use that word, concur, while she looks at a dead body. We all three probably need to get laid. I'm thinkin'...we all tried to peek at poor Mr. Casteel's privates...

and that's just wrong. Melody, you wash your hands entirely too often. Now, do either of you want fries with that?" Grace pulled her shirt over her mouth—she was beginning to taste the death.

"I don't even know how she knew the thing about 'hat man', but she's right. The getting' laid thing, I do concur. I may have glanced in the directions of his privates, Grace, but not in a perverted way...geeze!" Rikki said.

"Hat man?" Melody questioned. "Oh, and I concur...the laid thingy...too, also, as well." She giggled. "Excuse me Mrs. Lincoln, the shooting aside – how did you like the play?"

After that off-the-wall comment, Rikki looked sideways at Melody and frowned with a smirk. *Just let that one go.* "I saw a man wearing a baseball hat at the crime scene."

"Sometimes I don't know where one of you ends and the other begins. Good thing you came when you did...his wife, and attorney, I think, are coming to claim the body this afternoon." Melody added.

"Now you have Rikki's full attention, her eyes are big and she's about to ask you, when, where, who, what, how and why." Grace quickly said with her eyes still squeezed shut.

"Yeah, that!" Rikki was excited.

Melody laughed at Grace's good instincts. "Now I know why you bring her, she knows you better than you know yourself. I don't have an exact time but his wife, Lyric, I think was her name, said they would arrive in Tulsa around one, so it will be after that..."

Rikki grabbed Grace's arm. "*Wa-do* (thank you), Melody! Please don't mention that we were here, okay?" She pulled Grace toward the door.

"I never do, doll. Come see me soon." Melody zipped Miles Casteel's body bag and shoved him back into the drawer.

Outside Rikki took a deep breath with the belief it would cleanse her lungs of the dead people air. Grace jerked the goggles off her face and wiped her upper lip with her shoulder.

"We get to meet Lyric and Gates Linvick!" Rikki couldn't conceal her excitement.

"And I get to spend the day with you and your adrenaline rush without Ritalin. Great."

"Change in plans...we gotta get as much done as we can this morning. We will be on surveillance here at one o'clock." Rikki said after she jumped in the passenger's seat of the Mustang.

12

GRACE DRIVES LIKE A-U-LI-SI (grandma)...*don't say anything...let it go.* Rikki was a ball of energy—a need for speed pounded through her veins. *I should've driven...we'd be at the office by now. When are we gonna get there?* "It's the pedal on the right. You push it to go faster." The words fell right out of her mouth without even a warning.

"I'm not used to this car and you need to buckle up for safety. If you were buckled up I'd feel safer picking up speed. Since your not, I feel it is my duty to go just below the speed limit."

"What a crock a shit!" Rikki wasn't buying it. This was so typical of Grace.

"Time we put the cuss bucket back into effect. Your mouth is getting filthy again." Grace was a pro at disarming Rikki when she got like this.

Rikki dialed Gabriela, the interpreter. She agreed to meet them at the office in thirty minutes. *I'll make my players list at least this won't be a total waste of time.* She'd do anything to pick up the pace of the ride, and the investigation. A player's list was like organizing all your puzzle pieces before putting it together. Without fail, she always made one. This time her list consisted of the following players:

Jade Brackin   Client
Mr. Brackin   Client's Husband (don't even know his 1st name)

Miles Casteel	Murder Victim, Client's Lover & Sister's Husband
Lyric Casteel	Murder Victim's Wife, Client's Sister, Has motive—Greed
Abner Stickels	PI (who hired him?) SUV blew up, got his butt kicked by a girl
????????????	Who planted the bomb and tracking device?
Gates Linvick	Victim's Attorney
Hat Man	Who is he? What's his connection with the murder?

"Hey, Rikki, what if the office door explodes when we open it, like the SUV did?" Grace had both hands on the steering wheel, leaned slightly forward and wouldn't take her eyes off the road. She still had the outline of goggles on her forehead, around the sides of her face and on her upper lip.

"Have a little faith in me, would ya? We'll know if someone's jacked with the office doors. Besides, there was an officer positioned at our office last night. He was probably on the front side of the office but it should be all good." She didn't look up from her player's list. The list generated many more questions than answers.

"Toothpick or tape and hair? Or did you position the vase to break if someone touched the door knob?" Grace went through a few of Rikki's tricks.

"None of the above...a shotgun will fire and there will be a *u yo hu-sv* (dead) man at the back door. That will be our first clue that someone jacked with the door." She smiled proudly.

"Oh good God...help us all!" Grace didn't approve of the booby traps, but had to admit they have probably saved her life on occasion.

Grace visualized a dead body blocking the door as they neared the office. A knot formed in her gut and her foot let off the gas pedal. The car slowed and she turned into the parking lot. Grace forced her eyes to remain open. They wanted to slam shut so she didn't have to witness another dead body lying in a puddle of blood. Her head turned the opposite direction from the office building. She couldn't make herself look.

"Is it all clear?" She asked Rikki.

"Omigod! Who is that? I think it's a female...Gabriela! Gabriela jacked with the door!" Rikki yelled with conviction.

"Gabriela was shot? What are we gonna do?" Grace panicked. She swung her head around to view the tragic accident. There was no body or blood. "You are going to hell, Rikki Rankin! That was an evil thing to do!" Her panic turned to anger.

Rikki giggled, and then cackled, as Grace's reaction grew angrier. "Made ja look!" She got out of the Mustang and studied the door. "Stand to the side in case the shotgun goes off accidentally." She retrieved a thick string tucked under the threshold and pulled it upward. As long as the string couldn't move backward, under the door, the shotgun wouldn't go off.

Grace stepped to the side of the door and pressed her back against the building. She put her fingers in her ears and scrunched her face tight so the slightest bit of light couldn't penetrate her eyes, then she prayed. Rikki unlocked the door, unwired the shotgun and stuck it under her arm. She flipped on her office light and looked back down the hall. *Grace must still be standing out there with her fingers in her ears. Giggle. Guess the nice thing to do would be to go get her.*

Rikki stuck her head out the door. "Hey! It's *ni-ga-na-ye-gv-na* (safe)." She yelled at Grace, still standing in the exact spot and position.

"Oh, okay." Grace pulled her fingers out of her ears, opened her eyes and nonchalantly entered the office. All in a day's work.

***

Rikki, Grace and Gabriela arrived at the Downtown Hotel. The Mexican lady was to meet them on the ninth floor.

"So how's your love life, Gab?" Rikki asked in the elevator.

"I don't know. I think something's wrong with me. Out of the clear blue I tell my boyfriend, 'I think we shouldn't see each other anymore. I get bored or something."

"You spend too much time with Rikki." Grace interjected.

"We haven't found that special someone yet. It will take a 'hell of a man' to be able to put up with either of us." Rikki grinned.

"I know, right?" Gabriela agreed. "I don't want to be a slut so I stay with the same guy but I'm not in love." They laughed.

"You don't have to be a slut, Gabriela. Just say no to sex. How will you find that hell of a man if you're tied down to one you don't love?" Rikki asked.

"So is that what you do? Just say no to sex?" Grace asked.

The elevator doors opened on the ninth floor. "Of course it is." Rikki answered without looking at either of them and exited the elevator.

"For the love..." Grace uttered under her breath.

"Whatever." Gabriela said.

"What's this lady's name?" Rikki focused on the investigation again.

"Maria." Gabriela answered.

"I should've guessed that. How come so many Mexican women are named Maria?" Rikki looked around for Maria. She wasn't anywhere in sight. The cleaning cart wasn't anywhere on the floor either. She was supposed to be cleaning the rooms on the ninth floor. Rikki got a bad feeling in the depths of her stomach. 'The Gut Thing', she called it.

"It's ten o'clock she should be here. The cart is not even in the hall. It should be in the hall. Come on let's go." Rikki went to the service elevator and punched seven. She slid her 9mm out of its holster. Gabriela's eyes enlarged and she filled her lungs with too much air. Grace sighed.

The doors parted and Rikki had her gun pulled up to her shoulder with both hands. A slight hesitation before she exited the elevator. "Stay here." She whispered. The immediate area was secure so Rikki accelerated down the hall. There wasn't a doubt in her mind that evil lurked about, she felt it all through her body. The more intense the feeling became the more rapidly and warlike she raced down the hall. Never back down.

Grace and Gabriela watched Rikki disappear around a corner. The gun blasts made them dive to the floor and grab their ears. Grace had flashbacks of a few days earlier. *What if Rikki got shot this time?* When the gunfire ceased, Grace ran around the corner to find Rikki.

Neither Grace nor Gabriela was prepared for the blood bath display when they rounded the corner. Hat man lay in the middle of the hall covered in enough blood for two people. Blood splattered over the walls from the four rounds Rikki remembered firing. It could be more like nine, she wasn't sure. Rikki leaned against the wall with her head down taking deep breaths. The sudden rush of a life or death situation was exhausting.

"This can't be good." Rikki said. She looked at the body sprawled out before her. "He was already covered in blood before I shot him. Maria's got to be around here somewhere and it won't be pretty. Do you concur?" Rikki looked at Grace.

Gabriela leaned against the wall, her face bloodless and a grayish-white color. Grace recognized the signs—she was going to pass out. "Gabriela, you need to sit down and put your head between your legs. Rikki, you don't have to say concur just because there's a dead body." Grace glanced again at the body in the hall and shook her head.

Gabriela slithered down the wall, landed on the floor and tucked her head between her legs. "This is not happening." She began to cry.

"Oh, Rikki, press is going to eat you alive." Grace could already hear the news stories. "You've shot two men in what? Two or three days?"

"He had a fricking knife running at me...what was I suppose to do? I'm pissed right now...no, I'm *really* pissed. I gotta find Maria. Y-all can stay here or go to the elevator or come with me, I don't care." She approached the bloody body in the middle of the hallway and felt for a pulse. Nothing. *Good.*

Grace helped Gabriela steady herself and they followed Rikki down the hallway. She was the one with gun, better safe than sorry. *Who should we call first? I hope Rikki don't get in huge trouble for this. They will see her as unstable.* Grace worried.

"Should I call someone?" Grace asked.

"In a minute, let's find Maria. I'd also like to search hat man...that sounds like all kinds of wrong, but he's already dead, nothin' anyone can do for him now." Rikki had no remorse. *Tsi-i-hu* (killing) *man number two was much easier. I should probably run from myself.* She wanted this investigation to be over already. Nothing was going to hamper that determination. Rikki went straight to the crime scene to look for Maria. The door was locked.

"How are we going to get...?" Gabriela started to ask the question. Rikki pulled the card Rocky had given her out of her back pocket and stuck in the slot. The light turned green and the door opened. "Nevermind."

Maria was already dead. Her throat had been slashed. Her lifeless body tossed on the blood soaked bed without regard. The eerie look in Maria's opened eyes made Rikki want to throw-up. Grace gasped for air and Gabriela threw-up in the bathroom.

"This is horrendous." Rikki muttered under her breath. "He was gonna kill her anyway. So, don't y-all think this is our fault in any way."

"I'm guessing it already crossed your mind?" Grace asked.

"Only for a second. He probably would've killed her earlier if Rocky and I hadn't interrupted." Two deaths were enough to be responsible for. "They need to burn this room and never let anyone stay here again."

"Should we make those calls now?" Grace asked.

"Yup." Rikki dreaded what was to come. "Don't think I'll mess with 'hat man's' body...believe I've done enough for one day. There had to be something this guy was looking for at the crime scene. Could be the flash drive but what if it's something else?" She looked around the room again. The bottom drawer on the nightstand was pulled slightly out. *I know there was a coffee cup behind that drawer. Purdy sure I closed it all the way.* She retrieved a towel out of the bathroom before touching the drawer that was now covered in blood splatter. With the drawer out she squatted as low as she could and turned her head sideways, without actually putting her head on the floor. She held her hair up around the other side of her face. At this angle, she could smell the blood. *Sick.* She put her hand over her mouth and nose and gagged. She reached for what looked like a nickel.

"Frickin' button, probably there for two years." She crammed it in her pocket considering it now had her fingerprints on it. "Let's get out of here this room is creepy!"

Rikki raised and turned, she was alone in the room talking to herself. Grace and Gabriela were in the bathroom. Gabriela was a bit hysterical but doing a good job controlling it.

"I want out of here!" She yelled through tears at Rikki.

"Why are in you two bound to the bathroom?"

"Um, dead bodies, Rikki! Can't go in the room...dead body! Can't go into the hall...dead body! Who knows what's lurking around this place. I want out!" Gabriela put her hands over her face.

"Come on." Grace took Gabriela by the arm. Rikki led them out of the room and down the hall beyond the dead body to the elevator.

"You guys wait for me in the lobby. I've gotta stay here until TPD arrives to secure the scene." Rikki lit a cigarette and meandered back to 'hat man'.

A double edge knife had fallen on the ground beside the body. It resembled something a sniper would carry. *Is 'hat man' a hit man? Did he kill Miles Casteel too? Maybe if I just pulled out his wallet and looked at his ID. I should take pictures.* Rikki snapped a few shots of the man's body with her cell phone. She ran down the hall to get photos of Maria. *Don't know what's so urgent, hat man's not gonna get up and walk away.* She slowed down to a trot.

On the way back to hat man she heard the elevator. Officer Stone Russell charged around the corner and halted at the sight before him. Rikki gave a wave and a sweet smile. At least he wasn't naked in her head this time.

"Oh, Rikki, this is not good! What the hell happened?"

Rikki didn't say a word. With one finger she motioned for him to follow her. They entered the hotel room and Rikki pointed at the bed that held Maria's body.

"I'm going to need your statement."

"Okay. Are you ready? I'm gonna give it to ya right now. The dead man in the hallway slit Maria's throat then charged at me with his bloody sniper knife. I shot him. End of story."

"Might be the end but it's not the beginning. What were you doing here? How do you know this woman's name is Maria?" Officer Stone Russell meant business.

"She's a Mexican woman. They are all named Maria." Giggle. "Um, well, I brought an interpreter to help me talk to this woman. We were gonna meet her on the ninth floor but she wasn't there, came down here to see if we could find her. Found her just like this." She shrugged her shoulders.

"Why were you meeting her?"

"Dang, Stone, I can't reveal everything! I might get arrested."

"Rikki, you better tell me or you'll be telling someone else that don't care about you."

"Gotta point. Earlier this morning the dead man pushed the dead woman into me when I was searching the crime scene. He ran away and I arranged to meet Maria with an interpreter. And that is the entire story."

"I'm gonna go now." *Before you want a statement from Grace and Gabriela.*

"Guess I should ask how you are."

"*A-ya o-s-da* (I'm fine), gotta lot on my mind and I need to go. I stayed until someone got here to secure the scene." She didn't linger any longer.

"Rikki, you can't leave! It won't look good if you leave."

"You know where to find me." She disappeared in the elevator.

The lobby buzzed with police officers and homicide detectives arriving. Grace and Gabriela were seated near the door, not speaking, watching all the commotion. Rikki didn't break her stride as she walked near the seating area. "Let's get outta here, *a-ge-lv* (ladies)." Grace and Gabriela sprung to their feet and fell in behind Rikki, straight out the door.

The front of the hotel was decorated with police cars, their lights swiveled over the building. News stations parked their vans behind the police cars and set-up their satellites for live broadcast.

"Man, they're fast getting to a scene." Grace commented.

"We need to be invisible right now." Rikki looked for a way around the news teams. "Come on, this way." They disappeared around a pillar and to the side of the building. The three crawled over a four-foot cement wall and into the parking garage. "I have no idea where we are. Where'd we park?" Rikki was turned around.

"Where's the entrance?" Grace tried to get her bearings straight.

"I think we parked on the third level." Gabriela enlightened them.

"No way to go but up then." Rikki took off running up to the third level of the parking garage. Grace and Gabriela followed suit. They weaved in and out of the parked cars staying out of sight as much as possible.

"We should be on the seventh level by now. I'm so out of shape," Gabriela panted to get her breath.

"We're only on the second level, Gab." Grace giggled.

"Grace hit the gitter-inner...let's make sure the car's not parked on this level." Rikki looked for flashing lights among the parked cars while Grace pushed the car remote. Nothing. "Heave-ho let's go...it's not here." They ran to the next level. "Hit it again, Grace. Make it honk or something." They heard a faint honk in the distance.

"We're headed in the right direction." Grace was relieved.

All three of them were panting. Their pace had stalled to a fast walk up to the third level. An on-coming car gave them reason to stop behind a truck and hide, briefly. The car faded away and break-time was over. They took off again with an end in sight. Grace hit the remote one last time for an exact location of the Mustang.

"There it is!" Gabriela was glad to have the car in her sight, nine cars away from an escape.

"Thank God!" Grace saw the car too.

Teryn Tennin emerged from behind a cement pillar. "Hi Rikki. I was hoping to run into you...Don't shoot!" She raised her hands. Rikki pointed a 9 mm at her while she processed who was standing in front of her out of nowhere.

Rikki slid the gun back in the holster. "I'm guessin' you want an interview?" Rikki looked at Grace. Grace shook her head. She thought it was a good idea for Rikki to tell her side, once again. "Where's your camera crew?"

"I'll call them. It will only take a second." Teryn was already dialing. "I knew you wouldn't walk right out in the middle of the chaos down there, so I waited here in the parking garage." She began talking on the phone. "Hey, grab the camera and meet me on the third level of the parking garage. Yes. Let me ask her." She turned the phone upside down still against her ear. "Rikki, can we do this on the first level? He's afraid we won't feed into the live satellite."

"Sure. We will meet you down there." Rikki turned toward the Mustang. "I'm gonna drive this time." She said to Grace.

"Somehow, I figured that." Grace was already at the passenger's side door.

By the time they reached the first level the crew was ready to roll camera. Gabriela stayed to the side out of the camera's view. Rikki and Grace stood with Teryn waiting for the cue to begin the interview. Three, two, one....

"I'm here with Detective Rikki Rankin and her assistant Grace Michaels at the Downtown Hotel. Rikki, can you tell the viewers what happened?" Teryn moved her microphone toward Rikki and Grace.

"Well, Teryn, we were supposed to meet someone here for an interview regarding a homicide case we're working. We walked into a gruesome scene. Once again, I was forced to protect myself, Grace and this time, Gabriela." Rikki was matter-of-fact.

"Grace, did you see what happened?"

"I did, Teryn, but I don't think it would be appropriate to go into specific details at this time." She smiled politely at the camera.

"You've had a couple of trying days, to say the least. How are you holding up?"

"It has been trying, we are just doing our job and some days are worse than others. Honestly, I could've gone the rest of my life without the experiences of the last few days but what doesn't kill us makes us stronger, right?" Grace smiled at Teryn.

"Good attitude." Teryn smiled at Grace and directed her next question to Rikki. "What did the perpetrator say to indicate your lives were in danger?"

"Nothing. He didn't have time to say anything. He brought a knife to a gunfight and he lost. It wasn't just the knife he had that made me shoot him, you have to understand, it was the way he was charging at me and the blood all over his clothes and the knife. I knew he had already killed someone. We weren't going to be his next victims." Rikki's cell phone blared the song *Get A Rhythm* by Johnny Cash, she looked at it and said, "excuse me...I need to take this call." She stepped back away from the microphone and turned her back toward the camera.

Teryn began filling the airwaves with an update on the breaking news until Rikki finished her phone call. "I'm Teryn Tennin coming to you live from the Downtown Hotel where police are on the scene of a homicide and a self-defense shooting. We have just heard from Detective Rikki Rankin and her assistant Grace Michaels. You heard it first right here that a man charged at Rikki, Grace and a third person, with a bloody knife and was shot and killed by Detective Rankin. This is the second man in a matter of a few days that has challenged the pair and lost. If you recall Rikki shot Greg Hayes just three days ago." Teryn took a breath and continued talking.

Grace kept an eye on Rikki and didn't hear a word Teryn was saying. Rikki hung up the phone, turned to look at Grace with a bewildered look in her eyes. Grace knew something was very wrong.

Rikki walked up to Teryn and interrupted her. "Sorry Teryn, *o-ste-ga* (we are going)."

"Did you find out new information?" Teryn instinctively asked.

"Yes, but we have no comment." Rikki, Grace and Gabriela raced to the Mustang and took off.

"What was that call?" Grace asked immediately when the car was in motion.

"Tad Brackin is 'hat man'. Brackin...Jade Brackin, our client... what's the connection? Has she ever told you her husband's name?" Rikki couldn't get it out fast enough.

"Uumm, yeah she has...its Tad." Grace was in shock. Rikki had shot and killed their client's husband that was supposed to be out of the country.

"Damn. I was afraid you'd say that." Rikki shook her head.

13

At THE OFFICE THE phones were haywire. Rikki and Grace's cell phones were no better. Gabriela had already departed their company, she had all the hubbub she wanted for the rest of her life. Rikki and Grace couldn't get to the equipment room quick enough to escape the constant ringing. Grace entered the code to open the door, before it unlocked Lexi scampered down the hall.

"Hey guys! What's the deal? I saw you on the news! You hired me to do a job and I'm here to do it." She threw her purse atop her desk.

"Grace, I forgot about Lexi." Rikki whispered.

"Me too." Grace whispered back.

"Lexi! Boy are we glad to see you!" Rikki yelled.

Lexi was already answering the phone lines. "No comment at this time. I can take a message and have one of them call you back."

"I'm so glad she came to work!" Grace was impressed.

"Let's send out a text to everyone. Maybe that will slow down our cell phones a tad." Rikki suggested. She opened her phone; she had already received sixty-one texts. "Wow! I don't have time to read all these!" Her cell phone rang again. "It's Rocky, I'm gonna answer this one."

She lingered in the hall and flipped her phone open. "Hey, it was 'hat man' that I shot and guess who he turned out to be? My client's husband!"

"So I take it you're fine?" Rocky asked.

"*A-ya o-s-da* (I'm fine). Do people think I'm crazy?"

Rocky laughed. "I do, not sure about anyone else. Ya know, even with the beat up face you still looked sexy on TV. Do you wanna go to dinner later?"

"Sure, maybe even a little bit of yee-haw in the hay?" Giggle, "Can I just call ya? I have no idea what's gonna happen now."

Rocky laughed, "That's fine, baby. I can pick you up at your office if you want me to."

"That'll work. See ya later." Rikki entered the equipment room.

"Bye." Rocky said.

"Grace, you have to tell Jade about her husband, you've bonded with her." Rikki blurted when she saw Grace sitting at the counter.

"What? Why me? You know I don't like to be the bearer of bad news! I'll be there with you while you tell her but I just can't be the one to say it. Please, don't make me." Grace pleaded.

"But you have the bond...she's scared of me. Please, Grace, how is it going to sound if I blurt out *I shot your husband*? You're more compassionate, you have to." Rikki pleaded back.

"We both need to do it." Grace compromised.

"The sooner the better, huh? If we hurry we can make it back to the morgue before one. Then we can go to the hotel and break the news to Jade. I'll drive."

They locked Lexi in the office to man the phones. Rikki drove like a bat out of hell, no different than any other day. Grace opened the laptop and prepared to view the flash drive found at the crime scene.

"I feel like I haven't had a minute to really focus on this case. It appears that Tad Brackin is the murderer...but I don't think so. There's something botherin' me...I'm not sure what it is." Rikki said, actually thinking out loud.

Grace knew she didn't want a response. "I'm purdy sure Rocky feels like a yo-yo. You really need to shit or get off the pot with him."

"What? Where did that come from?" Rikki asked.

"Are you gonna see him tonight?" Grace already knew the answer.

"Well, yeah."

"See, shit or get off the pot. You like him one minute, the next minute you don't."

"I know. It's like I'm constipated when it comes to Rocky. I can't shit or get off the pot." Rikki laughed, hard. Grace did too.

"After all these years, I've never heard you describe a relationship quite like that. Just when I thought I'd heard it all." She wiped tears from her eyes and focused on the computer.

Embracing on the computer screen was Miles and Jade. It could've been a brother and sister hugging, not an intimate, lovers kind of hug. Grace studied it a minute, turned the screen to show Rikki. Rikki looked at it for a second, and then shrugged her shoulders.

"That's definitely not worth killing someone over. I don't get it." Rikki said.

Grace opened the next file on the flash drive. A photo of Jade, dressed in a formal gown, sitting at a fancy table probably a fundraiser event. The next several files were the same type of photos. Grace opened the last file. It was Miles' most recent will and testament.

"Wonder if this has anything to do with his murder? It's his new will." Grace said.

"I didn't think anyone knew about that though. Jade just found out yesterday. That makes me think his wife might be involved. She's the one losing out on millions. She's been my main suspect all along actually." Rikki answered.

"We're fixin' to meet her." Grace felt a rock forming in her stomach.

"I can't wait!" Rikki started to get excited. "What does Tad have to do with all this? Something Jade said to me is coming to mind…she said…It all boils down to money. There's too much involved in getting a divorce so we live our separate lives and stay married. It's never been a problem. She also said its more a marriage of convenience. So why was he here in Tulsa and not out of the country? Why did he kill Maria?" Rikki wanted answers.

"Good questions. How do you plan to find the answers? Apparently, Tad had a secret life." Grace shut the laptop computer and laid it in the back seat.

They rode in silence the rest of the way to the morgue. Rikki pulled into a parking spot and turned off the engine. They arrived before one—they waited in silence. Five minutes crept by and Grace couldn't stand the silence any longer.

"What are you pondering on so intently? Trying to figure Tad out?" She blurted.

"Naw. I was pondering Rocky Payne." She smiled.

"Wow! I'm in shock right now. You…thinking about a man… during an intense investigation. You care for him there's no other explanation." Grace didn't expect that from Rikki.

"Don't make more of it than it is, Grace. We are going on a date tonight…I was thinking about the yee-haw in the hay afterwards." She lied. She did care for Rocky but wasn't ready to admit it.

"You're such a horn-dog!" Grace snarled.

Rikki laughed, she loved getting to Grace. Of course, she had to take it one step further, "I love to be thrown around like a rag doll. He's real good at that…mmmmm…can't wait."

"Uh-huh, I like that too." Grace agreed, knowing it would shut Rikki up if she didn't get a response.

"Let's go on in. They should be here anytime." Rikki suggested.

"There is no reason we have to see any dead bodies, right?" Grace dreaded it.

"The only reason I can think of is that we are in a frickin' morgue! It's possible we will see death being wheeled by on a gurney." Rikki said sarcastically.

"You do need to get laid." Grace snapped.

Rikki giggled under her breath, "Shut-up."

"You shut-up." Grace was irritable at the thought of going back inside the morgue.

"Make me." Rikki kept the sparring alive. It helped Grace cope in this situation. "You need to get laid too." She opened the door and went inside. Grace didn't respond. She had her shirt pulled up over her mouth and nose.

They stood inside the door of the empty morgue. Melody was not anywhere insight. "It's like a ghost town in here." Rikki laughed at her intended pun. Grace tried not to.

"I was just thinking how you killed yet another man a few hours ago, and we were just talking about getting laid. Does that seem wrong?" Grace said from under her shirt.

"I still don't know what to do after killing someone. Should we have another party? I don't think it's wrong that we carry on with our lives as normal...I mean...he made me shoot him. I'm not a cold-blooded killer. Cold-blooded killers carry on like nothing happened after they murder someone. Oh dear, I don't like that resemblance!" Rikki shuttered at the epiphany.

"Don't compare yourself to a murderer, Rikki! There's a huge difference between self-defense and killing for the sport of it. If Melody really is asleep in one of the drawers I will pee my pants."

"I could see myself becoming a vigilante, just killin' bad guys for the sport of it. The world would be a safer place." Rikki said as they walked through the morgue searching for Melody.

"Rikki, never say that out loud again." Grace was concerned. "They'd lock you up and throw away the key and I wouldn't come visit you."

"It's in the vault...I'll never mention it again. She just might be in a drawer, I don't see her anywhere." Rikki visualized Melody sleeping in a drawer wrapped in blankets.

Down the hall and to the left they found her in an office asleep in a chair. Her neck appeared to be broken the way it was bent back and hanging to one side. They heard the door open. Rikki grabbed Melody's white lab coat from the coat rack and put it on.

"Today the part of Melody will be played by Rikki Rankin." She said to Grace. "Stay in here and don't let her come out of this room." She walked out to greet Gates and Lyric.

"You can't do that...let's wake her up." Grace half-heartedly tried to stop her, but she was already gone. *How do I always get thrown into these situations?*

"Good afternoon, how may I help you?" Rikki was all business. She scrutinized the pair, dressed in high-dollar attire, poised and polite, a bit solemn. Definitely rich folk from New York that put themselves above everyone else. *They think they are smarter than us hillbillies from Oklahoma...welcome to my world assholes.*

"Good afternoon. We're here for Miles Casteel." Gates said.

"I'm Melody, and you are?" Rikki said.

"I'm Gates Linvick, a longtime friend and attorney for Miles. This is Lyric Casteel, his wife." His introductions seemed arrogant to Rikki.

"I'm very sorry for your loss. Can I just get you to sign in over here?" Rikki knew the routine all too well. *Exactly what drawer is Miles in? Think...where were we...it's one of two. He was about waist high so it has to be the second one.* She hoped she was right.

"Can we make this as brief and unpretentious as possible?" Gates said in a demanding sort of way. Rikki didn't like him already.

"I'm always quick and easy...or brief and unpretentious... however you wanna say it." She locked into a stare down with Gates, to let him know he wasn't running the show, she was. He got the message but didn't like it. Rikki didn't like the look in his eyes. "Right this way." She led them to the drawer with Miles Casteel's body and pulled it out.

Lyric covered her face with her hands. "Oh God." She said and buried her face in Gates' shoulder. He wrapped his arms around her.

They seem a little too cozy. "I would assume that was a positive I.D. This is the man that you know as Miles Casteel?" Rikki was cold and calculated.

"Yes." Gates was just as cold and calculated.

Lyric turned back toward the body and slowly moved her hands away from her face. "I'm so sorry." She whispered.

Rikki wasn't going to let that comment go. "Why are you sorry, Mrs. Casteel?"

"I'm sorry this happened to my husband." She didn't make eye contact.

"You make it sound as if you had something to do with his murder."

"I didn't mean it like that. I'm sorry he had to suffer." She defended her comment.

"If it's any consolation, he didn't suffer." Rikki offered.

"And how would you know that?" Gates spoke down to Rikki.

"I would be happy to explain it to you, but I'm sure you really don't want to know all the details. The explanation would get a little gory. There's some paperwork you will need to fill out before we can release the body." Rikki shoved the drawer closed.

"It suddenly became real." Lyric said putting her hands back over her face then dragging them through her light brown hair. Rikki watched her reaction—fake reaction as far as she was concerned. There were no tears, no shaky voice, and no weak knees. When most people lose a loved one and see the body for the first time it can be chaotic.

"You can have a seat over here and I'll get the paperwork." Rikki directed them to a couple of chairs out of the way.

"Do you have his personal property, like his wallet, clothes and such?" Gates asked.

"Yes we do, I'll get them." Rikki disappeared into Melody's office.

"What's going on out there?" Grace whispered.

"They identified the body, now Gates wants his personal belongings." Rikki answered while she searched for Miles' bag of personal items. "Poor Mel, she's exhausted." Rikki paused a moment and looked at her. "Should we do something with her head? That's gonna hurt later."

"Just find what you're looking for so we can get out of here." Grace was nervous.

"Wait, I think there's a room where they store all the personal property. I'll go look." Rikki rushed out of the office. She located the property room further down the hall. It was fairly empty so she quickly found Miles Casteel's bag of belongings.

"Here you go. Everything he had on his person will be in there." She handed the bag to Lyric, not Gates.

Gates took the bag from her and tore it open. He rummaged through it. "This is everything?"

"Yes." *That's what I just said.* "Why? Is something missing?" Rikki pried.

"It's not important." Gates wasn't going to confide in her.

"Alright...well, just have a seat and someone will be with you to fill out the paperwork." Rikki had a gut-thing. She needed to get out of there. From halfway down the hall she turned back toward Lyric and Gates, there was one last question she had to ask. "I'm sorry, I almost forgot. Are you two having an affair?" She asked as if it wouldn't offend them.

Lyric couldn't control the guilt on her face when she jerked her head to the left to look at Gates. Gates couldn't speak—his jaw dropped and eyes dilated. Rikki noticed a flaming red tint to his face as well.

"That's what I thought." Rikki continued down the hall to get Grace and disappear.

"She hasn't budged." Grace updated Rikki on Melody's condition.

"Good. They can wait until she does. Let's fly!" Rikki took off the lab coat and replaced it on the coat rack. "We'll use the side door."

"Why? What did you do?" Grace was concerned.

"Nothin'." Rikki's voice was much higher than normal.

"Oh, yes you did! I can tell when your voice raises forty octaves that you are lying, you've done something!" Grace moved swiftly toward the side door. She knew when it was time to fly.

14

THE MUSTANG WHIPPED INTO the valet parking at the hotel around two-thirty. It was time to tell Jade about her husband. Rikki wasn't going to say a word. Grace would have to do it. *I'll just keep my mouth shut and give a compassionate look every once in awhile.*

"I still need to speak with that Abner dude." Rikki blurted.

"I totally forgot about him. I don't know how...every time I look at your fat lip I throw up a little bit in my mouth." Grace replied.

"Rocky thinks it's sexy." Rikki grinned.

Grace rolled her eyes, "He's just lying to you to make you feel better."

"Can I have more naproxen?"

"I'm wondering if you should go to the doctor."

"Hell no! Shut your pie hole! I don't need no stinking doctor." Rikki refused. "Do we need a plan? How are you gonna approach this topic?" They got off the elevator and walked down the hallway to the hotel rooms.

"Me? We both will do it. Jade is going to be so shocked that you shot her husband. This is awful. How did this happen?" Grace's anxiety was out of control.

"We need to remain calm. Keep our voices soft and be sympathetic."

"Is this something you need to practice? Or, will it come natural?" Grace asked.

"Hateful, it will seem natural."

"That's what I thought. Ok, here we go." Grace opened the door. "It's us!"

Jade sat in a chair at the round table positioned by a window. Johnny holstered his gun and sat back down in a chair opposite Jade.

"Hello, ladies." Jade was glad to see them. She had been so bored, stuck inside with this mass of muscle that never spoke.

"Hello." Grace was grim.

Rikki nodded in her direction.

Johnny looked up briefly saw the look on Rikki's face and knew something was up. He looked down at the floor and waited for the bomb to hit.

"Jade, we need to talk to you." Grace began and then looked at Rikki for her to pick up the story. Rikki didn't say a word. She only looked at Jade with what she thought was sympathy. Grace was furious. "There was an accident at the hotel." She nervously continued.

Rikki had already heard enough. "It wasn't an accident, Grace. It was on purpose. Jade, look...your husband, Tad, came at me with a bloody knife. I shot him. He didn't make it. I'm so sorry." Rikki wrapped it up in a matter of seconds. "He wasn't out of the country. He was right here in T-town. He also stabbed a Mexican woman to death."

"What? Tad is dead?" Jade slumped in her chair. "That lying son-of-a-bitch!" She screamed.

Grace couldn't speak. She looked at Rikki in disbelief. *Unbelievable. I'm not seeing the natural sympathy here.*

Johnny's eyebrows rose to mid-forehead. He didn't budge. He wanted to hear this.

"That's it, just let it out." Rikki said to Jade. "He's a lyin' sack of crap!"

"Did he kill Miles?" Jade asked, ignoring Rikki's comments.

"I don't know yet. I'm not ruling him out as a suspect, that's for sure. I did meet Gates and your sister. They were at the morgue identifying Miles. You should call them and see if they are gonna read the will. You need to be there when they do. I'd be happy to go with you. In the meantime, there are a few things I need to do." Rikki played her hand at being compassionate.

"So Tad brought a knife to a gun fight?" Johnny asked.

"Eww, you saw that?" Grace shuttered.

"Sure did. Then we watched the other channels. They are saying Rikki is trigger-happy...a vigilante...what was the other thing? Oh yeah, on a killing spree. Not good, not good at all." Johnny filled them in on the news reports.

"Rikki you gotta fix this! People are being killed; you are getting beat up and blown through the air from a bomb...what next?" Grace sat down on the bed and put her head between her legs. She was feeling light headed. "Hurry up and fix this."

"That's what I'm screamin'! Johnny, you think it's safe for you guys to stay here or should you move?"

"I think its fine for now. The focus seems to be on you."

Grace's cell phone rang. She was only on the line for a few seconds before hanging up. "I have to get to the office. Lexi is going nuts with all the reporters banging on the door and calling. She needs help."

"I'll drop you off. Hey, did you get Abner's cell phone downloaded? I need all the info I can get before I go talk to him." Rikki asked.

"Not yet. I can do it when we get back to the office."

"Who is Abner?" Jade asked.

"The dude that gave me this fat lip and a suspect. Remember?" Rikki answered.

Johnny smirked. "I'd like to have seen that."

"Is that right? Get up and I'll demonstrate what happened." Rikki took the fighting stance, ready to let Johnny have it.

"Stop it! We have to go!" Grace's patience was wearing thin.

"You got lucky, mister." Rikki pointed at Johnny with narrow eyes.

Johnny laughed. "Whatever."

"Don't *whatever* me!"

*****

Rikki and Grace didn't speak on the drive to the office. Rikki focused on Abner and his role in all this. Grace relived everything that had happened in the last seventy-two hours. It seemed like a year had passed. She prayed for their lives to get back to normal, their version of normal anyway. Rikki sailed through the office parking lot in the Mustang.

"I think it went well. Jade handled the news like a real sport." Rikki finally said.

"A real sport? What else could she do? You blurted it out like you were inviting her to a Tupperware party."

"I don't do Tupperware parties, Grace." Rikki laughed.

The front of the parking lot resembled a circus. Reporters crawled over each other like roaches. The front door was crowded with cameramen, cameras and microphones. Some were live on the air reporting the story, while others strategize what angle of the story they wanted to cover. The scene stunned Rikki and Grace.

"Omigod! Seriously Rikki, my butt hole just tightened and I feel like I could spit nails!" Grace's eyes filled with tears, she turned to Rikki for comfort.

Rikki had tears forming in the corners of her eyes too, but hers were from laughing at Grace. "Are you telling me your not gonna crap for a year?"

"If ever again." Grace was serious.

Rikki gained some composure as she pulled up to the back door. "I'm gonna drop you off and go find Abner. Will you call me with the four-one-one on his phone?"

"Yes. After I do that, Lexi and I are going home. We can't stay here in this chaos."

"You could open the front door and say we have no comment at this time. Maybe that would get rid of some of them. Or give them a statement." Rikki suggested.

"You need to do it. Why don't you?"

"I don't want to deal with it right now. I'll call Cliff and Katey and see if they want an interview in the morning. I only want to deal with people I trust."

"That would be good. At least on the radio the scabs on your chin won't show." Grace agreed.

"Give me a complex why don't you!"

Rikki dabbed ointment on her chin as she waited for Grace to get inside the back door. When she disappeared behind the door, Rikki took off to find Abner.

*****

The stench seeping from the jail cells made Rikki gag, possibly her least favorite smell ever. It had to be worse than the death smell at the morgue. Her lip curled up on one side while she tried to adjust to the stagnate aroma. *Creepy that live people can smell worse than the dead.* The jailer led her to Abner through the high security locked doors. They finally reached a room where Abner sat at a table alone.

"Do you need me to stay with you?" The jailer asked.

"No, that's okay." Rikki answered.

"I'll be right outside the door then."

"Thank you." Rikki smiled pleasantly.

"Did you come to shoot me too?" Abner mouthed off.

"Don't put it past me." She growled. "So if you weren't hired to kill Miles Casteel, who hired you and what for?" She got right to the point of her visit.

"I didn't kill Miles Casteel. And you should know as well as I do that I can't and won't tell you who my client is. Sorry you wasted your time." He stood his ground.

"Look, if you work with me, I'll see what I can do to get you out of here. Don't you want to know who killed Miles and blew your SUV to shreds?"

"What makes you think I don't already know?" Abner was cocky.

"Who hired you?" Rikki didn't let him play mind games.

"Can't tell you."

"Why is Lyric Casteel's number in your cell phone? And why have you had so many calls with her the last few weeks?" Rikki's demeanor began to change from let's work together; to I'm going to hang you out to dry. "That tells me pretty much without a doubt that she's your client. And she's been one of my main suspects. Where does that leave you?"

"You don't know what you're talking about." Abner remained calm. He wasn't going to let Rikki play mind games either.

"No? Then why don't you enlighten me." She had a cold stare embedded on him.

"I'm not telling you anything. I want to see if you can figure it out." He toyed with her.

"You're mad 'cause I beat the snot out of you. How are your balls anyway?" She toyed back. She knew she wasn't going to get anywhere with him.

"I'm through talking to you." He sealed his lips tight.

"Everything happens for a reason, Abner. If you hadn't been arrested you'd be dead right now. In essence I saved your life. So…you're welcome." Rikki tapped on the door for the jailer to let her out.

In the parking lot Rikki took a deep breath. *I want to see my kids and Rocky.* It was a little before five o'clock. *Time to call it a day and relax for a change.*

15

ON THE WAY TO see Gunner and Mallie at their dad's, Rikki called Katey. Katey was excited to hear from Rikki and they agreed to do an interview at the radio station in the morning. Gunner and Mallie met their mom at the door with fifty questions. Rikki answered them all and reassured them that she was fine and this would all be over soon. They were ready to be home with their mom, just as she was.

Rocky had been watching the news and told Rikki it was probably a good idea if they stayed in for the night. No telling what would transpire with her in a public place. She agreed. Rocky picked up Chinese food so Rikki wouldn't have to cook. Rikki drove to his ranch ready to relax.

She walked in without knocking, as she did most places she went. Rocky was in the kitchen getting plates and silverware ready. From the looks of the counter covered with Chinese boxes, he bought one of everything on the menu. *Him's cute.* She smiled at the sight of him. The outside world was a million miles away with Rocky in her vision. Immediately peace embraced her troubled soul.

"Hi, honey." She said softly, not wanting to disturb the calmness she felt.

"Hi. I didn't hear you come in." He smiled at her. He sat the plates on the counter and made his way to her. He scooped her up tightly in his arms and gently kissed her. It didn't matter to Rikki that her lip was swollen and sore, she craved his affection. "*Ja-yo-si-ha-s* (Are you hungry), sweetie?"

"Famished. I haven't eaten since we drove through Whataburger at four this morning." Rikki felt exhaustion trying to take over her body. She fought it of course. She didn't want to miss a minute with Rocky.

"We're ready to eat so go ahead and dig in." Rocky could tell by Rikki's actions that she was tired and stressed. He had many questions about the investigation but decided not to ask. She needed a break from it all.

Rikki fixed her plate with way too much food but she intended on eating every bit of it. "Do you wanna go with me in the morning to KTFX radio station? Cliff and Katey are going to interview me." She shoveled the Chinese food in her mouth. "Mmmm, there's a party in my mouth right now."

He laughed at her off the wall comment. "Sure, what time?" He asked and shoveled food in his mouth too.

"Seven." She said with her mouth full.

"That's early, it is, it is. But I guess I can manage it." He grinned at Rikki. She was mesmerized by his good looks and couldn't help but stare at him.

"You sure are being *u-ga-na-s-da* (sweet) for a change." She acknowledged his actions.

"You've had a rough few days. Since you're not whining about it I thought I would be nice." He teased.

"I don't whine!"

"Really?"

I love the way he says really. "See now you're not being sweet. I need you to be sweet." She was already feeling full and her plate didn't look like she'd even taken a bite. "I think I got way too much food."

"Ya think?"

"Stop it." She whined just a little.

"American or cheddar?" He gave her a hard time.

"I don't need cheese 'cause I'm not whining...you think I'm whining when I'm not, then you harass me until I do whine. I think you like it when I'm whiney."

Rocky laughed at how easy he could get under her skin and get a reaction out of her. "Come here." He pulled her close to him. Rikki closed her eyes and sucked in his smell, she loved the way he smelled.

"Are you done eating?" She whispered.

"I am."

"Let's spoon!" She loved to snuggle with Rocky.

"That's *kinda* what I was thinkin'." He raised his eyebrows.

Rikki laughed, "I know exactly what you're thinking...perv!" She reached up and kissed him softly, she wanted a good rough, passionate kiss but her lip was too sore.

"No you don't. Follow me." He took her hand and led her outside through the back door. "I made sure it is exactly one hundred four degrees."

He had prepared the hot tub for Rikki to relax. She wasted no time ripping off her clothes. The chill in the air immediately gave her goose bumps and sent her hopping across the deck to jump in the hot tub. Rocky watched her hourglass figure bounce toward the steamy water and giggled as he undressed then strutted across the deck unaffected by the chill.

Rikki positioned her back against a jet and watched the naked six foot four inch hunk of a man saunter toward her. Her body trembled with anticipation of him being next to her—touching her. Rocky had no interest in leaning against a jet. With a smirk on his lips and fire in his eyes he inflicted on Rikki. They floated in the water as he kissed her with intent. Their bodies brushed together in the current of the water. Rikki grabbed him and pulled him tightly against her body. She felt him throbbed against her wet skin.

"I'm sorry honey; I intended on letting you relax in the hot tub...not attacking you...but I can't help it."

"Shut-up." Rikki pulled him closer to her body again and pressed her lips to his.

Rocky couldn't contain his eagerness any longer. Rikki granted him access to have his way with her. He plunged into her against the gush of the water with ten times the force of the jets. At this very moment they were the only two in the world.

Both were content afterward as they relaxed in the hot tub until their skin wrinkled. "We better go in, it's getting late." Rocky suggested.

"You're right. We didn't bring any towels...this is going to be really cold!"

"Jump and run baby." Rocky thought it was funny.

"I'm right behind you."

Rocky got out of the hot tub then helped Rikki out. Their bodies dripped with water that cooled immediately. Rocky tugged Rikki by the arm and tucked her nude body against his. They ran inside leaving water tracks on the floor, straight to the bathroom to dry off. Once they were dry Rocky led Rikki to the bedroom. She didn't waste any time sliding between the sheets with Rocky right behind her. She pressed as close as she could against the warmth of his naked body. The warmth of his breath melted her heart. She didn't fight it this time. *Just roll with it, let it happen.* She coached herself.

He thrust his tongue in her mouth and slid his hand down her waist to her leg then back up the other leg lingering on her breast. Her back arched with pleasure and her breathing increased. She could feel his breathing quicken as she ran her hand down his stomach.

"Ding, ding, round two?" Rikki whispered.

"Just try and stop me."

They lay quietly in each other's arms after they made love. Rikki's mind was clear and she wasn't thinking about anything. The murder case was the last thing on her mind. She enjoyed the safety and peace she experienced with Rocky. She never wanted to forget this moment. She never wanted to leave this moment.

"That was incredible." She finally whispered.

"Yes, it was." Rocky savored the moment as well. He loved having Rikki next to him.

"*Wa-do.*"

"No need to thank me." He thought a thank you was absurd it was his pleasure.

"I mean for everything you do."

"Baby, I worry about you. You can get yourself in some real messes." He kissed her forehead.

"I don't want you to worry. I can handle myself." She closed her eyes.

"I know you can but still I worry."

"I'm sorry." She didn't know what to say to make it better.

"Just be careful. Don't get reckless, you promise?"

"I promise." She was so relaxed and in the moment. "I love you, Rocky." Her body stiffened at the sound of her own voice. She hadn't said those words to a man in fifteen years.

Rocky was silent. He wasn't sure if he heard her right. Once he was positive he did hear her correctly, he said, "I love you, Rikki."

Rikki concentrated on every inch of her skin that touched his. She embedded it in her brain so she could remember how incredible she felt at this very moment. They drifted quietly off to sleep.

16

THE ALARM BLASTED AT six o'clock, Rikki swatted at random things on the nightstand trying to make it stop. Rocky finally leaned over her and shut it off.

"*O-s-da* (good) morning, beautiful." He said.

"*O-s-da* (good) morning, handsome."

"Time for me to jump in the shower," she said with dread.

"Not so fast. You're not goin' anywhere!" Rocky held her down.

"Is that right? All of a sudden you're the boss of me?" Rikki teased.

"I've always been the boss of you. You always do what I say anyway...so what does that tell you?" He pulled her on top of him.

"I'm submissive I guess." She giggled.

"Whatever!" His deep laugh made Rikki shiver. "You are the furthest thing from submissive."

"*Tla yi-go-li-ga* (I don't understand)." She played innocent.

The passion picked up where it left off the night before. Thirty minutes later she forced herself away from Rocky and into the shower. She tried to focus on the interview but her mind couldn't stop replaying the activities of the last twelve hours. She felt alive like never before.

*****

At the radio station Cliff and Katey were already on the air doing the morning show. Rikki and Rocky entered the sound booth as they went to commercials. Cliff and Katey hugged Rikki and then Rikki introduced Rocky. Rocky and Cliff both stood six foot four inches tall and enjoyed being able to look each other in the eyes without looking down all the time. Rikki and Katey rolled their eyes at them as they did that male bonding thing.

"Rikki, how have you been? We watch the news and get furious at what all they are saying about you." Katey jumped right into the conversation.

"I'm great." She smiled and glanced at Rocky. "Never been better. I actually haven't seen the stories but I have heard. So let's get down and dirty on the air shall we?"

"Back-up sister. What's this? What's going on?" Katey pointed to Rikki then to Rocky. "I know you and this is not the norm."

"No it's not. I stepped outside my box a little." Rikki admitted.

"Hey, girls we got one minute." Cliff informed them.

"Where's my ear muffins?" Rikki asked.

"They're called headsets not ear muffins." Cliff corrected her.

"Your ear muffins are right here." Katey laid them out.

"Thank you."

"Oh, this is going to be fun. They always gang up on me when we do this." Cliff said to Rocky.

"Somehow that doesn't surprise me." Rocky said as he sat down behind Rikki.

"I promise we won't...we will be gentle. This isn't one of those fun interviews like usual," Rikki said.

Rikki, Cliff and Katey were seated in front of their microphones with their headsets on. This was Rocky's first experience in the studio and he beamed with pride as he watched Rikki.

"Thirty seconds." Cliff said.

"We need to get together for a cocktail or two." Rikki said to Katey.

"I know. I've been thinking the same thing. When do you want to go?" Katey said.

"Let's try one day this week. I like to say cocktail." Giggle.

"Girls, can we focus here?" Cliff interrupted. He pushed the on air button. "The All New Okie Country 101.7, continuous hit country, I'm Cliff..."

"And I'm Katey." Katey added.

"We'd like to welcome Private Detective Rikki Rankin. It's great to see you, Rikki." Cliff introduced Rikki.

"It's great to see both of you. Thanks for having me on this morning."

"You've been all over the news the last few days. What do you think about the reports?" Cliff asked.

"As you can imagine I'm not too happy about any of it. I have to keep in mind these reporters are trying to get ratings, and if that's at my expense they don't seem to care."

"The front page of the newspaper this morning says *trigger happy* and *out of control* with a picture of you. I have to tell you when I read it this morning it made me mad. I can't imagine how you felt." Katey said.

Rikki dug deep within her being to answer. "I haven't seen that. It makes me furious—to say the least. The focus needs to be on the bad guys, the guy responsible for killing Miles Casteel and Maria. The guy that put a bomb in a vehicle that shot me through the air. That's where the focus needs to be. Not the fact that I've shot two men in self-defense. I merely protected Grace, Gabriella and myself. Anyone in my shoes would've done the same thing." The anger in Rikki's voice was apparent. "The people writing all these fictitious reports better hope that I'm there to protect them or their loved ones if they're ever caught in a similar situation...evidently they wouldn't protect themselves. They'd just lie down and die. They need to ask themselves what they would do in my shoes."

"Or ask themselves...what would Rikki do?" Cliff added.

"I like that, what would Rikki do?" Katey said.

"That's funny, Cliff." Rikki tried to calm down. "I would protect those around me no matter what it took. So I don't care what they make up to say about me. I know the facts and if I hadn't shot those men...I wouldn't be here right now...that's the bottom line. I feel like the public in general is scared of me because of the reports...I've gotten some pretty unsettling reactions. Let me just say...there's no reason to be scared of me, if anything you should feel safe and sound. I would protect a total stranger exactly as I did Grace and Gabriella.

"I know that about you. What do you plan to do now?" Katey asked.

"I'm going to find the one responsible for murdering these innocent people, and make sure he or she pays. I don't care if the media respects that or not."

"We are behind you one hundred percent, Rikki." Cliff assured her.

"I know you will find the person that committed these heinous crimes and bring them to justice." Katey said.

"I appreciate you guys having me on this morning." Rikki said, "Letting me vent so to speak. I'm not a vigilante and I'm not trigger-happy or out of control. I am, however, on a manhunt to find the person or persons responsible and hold them accountable for their actions. If that makes me anything other than a respectable human being then so be it. They can say all the negative things they want about me. It will not stop me from bringing down the bad guys."

"If you just tuned in, we are speaking with Private Detective Rikki Rankin. She is setting the record straight regarding her actions of self-defense. If you find you are in a similar situation, remember to ask yourself, what would Rikki do?" Cliff reported. "Rikki, thank you for coming in and speaking with us here at The All New Okie Country 101.7, continuous hit country."

"*Wa-do* (thank you) Cliff and Katey for having me." Rikki said removing her headphones. She shook her head and fluffed her hair then looked at Rocky. "And that's a rap, we're done here."

"You did good." Rocky told her.

Cliff and Katey went to commercial so they could say goodbye to Rikki and Rocky. Cliff walked them downstairs so he could smoke a cigarette between airtime. "I will play that interview again tomorrow. I want to make sure you are heard." Cliff cupped his hand around his lighter to light his cigarette.

"I appreciate it." Rikki smiled. "I'll talk to you later." She crawled up in Rocky's truck as he held the door for her.

Rikki's cell phone began playing a song. *"My milkshake brings all the boys to the yard, and their like, it's better than yours. Damn right it's better than yours, I could teach you, but I'd have to charge..."*

"Whose ring tone is that?" Rocky frowned and smirked at the same time.

Rikki laughed, "It's Cricket." She flipped open her phone, "Hey!"

"What would Rikki do?" Her cousin Cricket laughed into the phone.

"You were listening?"

"I did. I'm so glad you did that! Now you need to schedule a press conference."

"I will. I've been running around like a lunatic on the loose! I know I do need to make time for a press conference. I just feel so misunderstood."

"Did you want me to call the waaa-mulance? Or are you gonna do something about it?" Cricket was to the point.

"Shut-up, I'm not whining, merely stating the facts."

"I can get you some Swiss." Rocky laughed.

"You shut-up too! What is wrong with you people?" Rikki said to both of them. "And if I did want to whine, you both would listen and be sympathetic!" She demanded.

"Dang your defensive!" Cricket said.

"Walk in my shoes for an hour...you would be too...omigod...I gotta go!" All the blood drained from Rikki's face, the pit of her stomach turned.

"You okay?"

"No, I'll talk to you later."

"Love you." Cricket was concerned.

"Love you, too." Rikki hung up and began fumbling with the buttons on her phone.

"What's wrong, baby?" Rocky watched her in a panic.

"I'm not sure. Something's not right. It just hit me...when Cricket said defensive." She pulled up the pictures she had taken of Tad lying in the hallway. She zoomed in on his hands. "That's what I was afraid of...defensive wounds on his hands. This changes everything." She tossed her phone on the console and put her face in her hands and rocked back and forth. "Omigod."

"What is wrong with you?" Rocky was confused.

Silence.

Rikki replayed the scene in her head of Tad charging toward her with the knife.

"Honey?"

"I've made a huge mistake, huge mistake." Rocky had never seen Rikki in such a panic before. Rikki couldn't call Melody at the morgue fast enough.

"This is Melody."

"This is Rikki. Do you have Tad Brackin?"

"Yes ma'am. He's right here. Did you need to talk to him?" Melody joked.

"I wish I could. Does he have defensive wounds on his hands?"

"Yes ma'am."

"Any stab wounds?" Rikki closed her eyes and braced herself for the answer.

"Two."

"Oh, no! I shot an innocent man!"

"He would've died from the stab wounds." Melody was matter of fact.

"So I put him out of his misery?"

"So to speak."

"Who knows this?"

"Nobody."

"He was running to me for help...not to attack me." Rikki whispered.

Rocky pulled over in a parking lot. He couldn't believe what he just heard.

"What are you going to do?" Melody asked.

"Right now...I'm dyin' a little bit on the inside. This can't get any worse. I'll call Officer Stone."

"I won't say anything until I hear from you again."

"Please don't let this out to the media." Rikki pleaded.

"I won't, doll. How were you supposed to know? You did what you thought you had to do." Melody tried to help.

"Thanks." Rikki's heart ached as if slashed by the knife. She focused on Rocky. He watched her with a blank stare, speechless.

"By the way, were you here earlier? Seems someone impersonated me."

"It was me. Can we talk about that later?" Rikki confessed.

"I don't know anyone else that would've done that so I figured it was you."

"Talk to ya later." Rikki hung up, still focused on Rocky. "There's someone out there killin' people like he's pickin' daisies." Rikki said to him. "This is only a speculation but I think Tad tried to help Maria and he got stabbed in the process. He was running for help when I shot him. Melody said he would've died from the stab wounds. It was fear and panic in his eyes, not evil." Rikki tried to explain to Rocky and make sense of it herself. She closed her eyes.

"I don't know what to say. I'm sorry." Rocky struggled.

"Trigger happy. Maybe they're right." Rikki beat herself up.

"You couldn't have known. What was he doing there anyway?"

"*That*, I do not know." She took a deep breath and slowly released it. "Grace is gonna freak. Officer Stone is really gonna freak! You know what this means? The perp was still there when I found Maria. He was still frickin' there. Unless he was on the other elevator when we arrived on that floor." Rikki tried to put it all together.

"What do you want to do now?"

"Let's go back to your house. I'll get my car and figure out what to do from there."

"I love you." Rocky softly said.

Rikki managed a smile, "I love you too." *Maybe everything will be all right after all.*

17

GUILT, REMORSE, SHAME, REGRET all engulfed Rikki at the same time. She was alone at her office and couldn't shake the clutch this case had on her. Her life would never be the same because of this case. Would she question her actions for the rest of her life? Would she ever forgive herself? *Lord, I know you have forgiven me, please let me forgive myself! Please give me strength, get me through this...carry me through this. Thank You for Rocky.* Rikki had prayed continuously since she left Rocky's house. *Things can't get any worse. What's my next move? What do I do?* She was on the verge of tears, but refused to let one fall.

Tad Brackin haunted her thoughts. She saw him coming at her over and over. The look in his eyes, it was evil. No matter how many different ways she replayed the horrific event it all ended the same. He was coming at her with the intent of killing her—she knew it. *If he was about to die, he may have been disillusioned; he may have gone after anyone in his path out of fear, out of his mind. He knew he had to fight he was in shock and bleeding to death. He did try to attack me there's not a doubt in my mind. The beast backed into a corner will always attack.*

Peace finally eased through her troubled spirit. Rikki came to a truce about the actions she had taken against Tad. She did what she had to do. Now if only the media didn't blow it out of proportion. *There is hope that they are none the wiser and it will* just go away. *Who am I trying to kid? I should address it before they do. Face it head on like it was common knowledge and they are the ones that screwed up by not knowing. I should call Grace.* She glanced at the clock it was eleven eleven. She called Grace.

"Good Morning." Grace said.

"Where ya at?"

"I'm right here."

"Ha ha, funny. Are you coming to the office? I have lots to tell you. A couple new developments."

"Really? Good or bad?"

"Both. When can you be here?"

"Give me an hour."

"K...bye." Rikki hung up. She lay on the couch in her office and updated her player's list. At least she did have a bit more information about this case.

Jade Brackin	Client
Mr. Brackin	Tad Brackin i.e. Hat Man – dead I killed him – tried to help Maria
Miles Casteel	Murder Victim, Client's Lover & Sister's Husband
Lyric Casteel	Murder Victim's Wife, Client's Sister, Has motive – Greed...suspect an affair with attorney Gates Linvick
Abner Stickels	PI (who hired him?) SUV blew up, got his ass kicked by a girl – wont talk...why? Lyric's phone number on his cell...she hired him... had to be her...he's not a killer...why'd she hire him?
???????????	Who planted the bomb and tracking device?
Gates Linvick	Victim's Attorney...suspect an affair with Lyric
Hat Man	See Tad Brackin.....

She read over the list at least a hundred times, with the hope something would click in her brain. Some connection, somewhere. *Think. What am I missing? The will...Gates knows about the will...I know about the will...Jade knows about the will... who else knows? It was on the flash drive. I need to get Lyric alone and interrogate the hell out of her. Jade needs to identify Tad's body...damn...I need to do a press conference...where's Grace? She should be here by now. Where's Lexi...I didn't fire her...did I? Hell, I don't even know what I'm doing. Focus Rikki...people are dying... and I've killed two of them...no don't think like that...a-gi-yo-si (I'm hungry). I need a Ritalin...I miss Rocky...him's cute. This is getting me nowhere.*

Rikki got up and paced. She had on the same jeans and shirt from yesterday. She wanted to change clothes but didn't feel she had the time. At least she showered. Finally, she heard Grace prancing down the hall.

"Good news or bad news?" She yelled.

"Bad." Grace yelled back.

"Tad had been stabbed twice before I shot him. He didn't kill Maria, but he was coming at me with the knife. He was in shock...Melody said he would've died anyway."

"That is some bad news." Grace was in Rikki's office planted on the couch, while Rikki paced. "Did you have a melt down?"

"I did, I'm over it. I don't doubt for a minute he would've killed me. Just one of those things. It freaked me out at first. I will mention it in a press conference like everyone should've already known about the stab wounds."

"You're doing a press conference?"

"Yes...will you set that up?"

"Geeze, I guess so. And the good news?"

"I stepped outside my lonely box. I decided to shit instead of get off the pot....so to speak. I said the 'L' word to Rocky." Rikki grinned.

Grace was shocked; she stared at Rikki for a minute. "Rocky? You are in love with Rocky? I had an idea but never thought you would act on it...what about Jaxon?" Grace always rooted for Jaxon.

"I never had a relationship with Jaxon. He is hot though. There's something about Rocky that just completes me...I'm calm around him. I don't know. I'm gonna try really hard to make this work. I'm not gonna sabotage it this time."

"I'll believe it when I see it. Well, I am happy for you."

"Thanks. Jade is gonna have to identify Tad's body. I'm gonna call Johnny and have him meet us at the morgue."

"I'm not going back to the morgue! The last time stressed me out." Grace was serious.

"Melody knows I impersonated her." Rikki laughed.

"Was she pissed?"

"I don't know...didn't act like it. But we were talking about Tad being stabbed."

"I'm gonna set-up the press conference for this afternoon if possible. Pretty sure they will all show up. You are still all over the news."

"I haven't seen any of it. Hey, did you hear me on the radio?"

"I did...what would Rikki do...that Cliff is so funny." Grace disappeared into her office to make the twenty phone calls.

Rikki made a few calls, one to her kids, one to Rocky, and one to Officer Stone Russell and one to Johnny. Johnny said they would meet at the morgue at four and he would check out of the hotel. He felt they needed to move Jade. Rikki agreed. Gunner and Mallie begged to come home. Rikki felt bad for them and arranged for Cricket to stay with them at home. Rocky said he would be at her office within the hour. He wanted to be there when she faced the press at the conference. Officer Stone Russell was just pissed. He'll get over it. Rikki should've called Officer Luke Hixon too but was tired of being on the phone.

"Two o'clock!" Grace yelled from her office. "The press conference is at two o'clock here."

"I'm gonna run home and change real fast." Rikki yelled back. "I've been in these clothes for two days. Do I smell?"

"I didn't smell you. Wear something girly, something not intimidating. You know what I mean? And take a Ritalin." Grace suggested, now standing in the doorway of Rikki's office.

"Gotcha." Rikki went to the kitchen and took a pill then ran home to change. She chose a pink shirt and dark brown vest with a pair of blue Levi's. She pulled her hair back and put on a small amount of make-up that covered the chin scab. Her fat lip looked much better and she was confident she would be able to pull this off without a hitch. She placed her gun in the usual spot.

The dirty jeans were thrown on the floor. Out of instinct she checked the pockets and recovered the button she found at the crime scene. *I forgot about this.* She put it in her pocket and ran out the door.

Back at the office Rocky patiently waited. Rikki threw herself in his arms and hugged him. "I needed that."

"You look gorgeous." He admired her.

"*Wa-do* (thank you)." They kissed.

Grace happened on them and spun around and left the immediate area. Not what she was in the mood to see. *He is a distraction to her right now. No wonder this case isn't solved yet.*

"Are you ready for this?" Rocky asked.

"Oh, sure. It's not my first rodeo, cowboy. I've had to do several press conferences. Well, none like this I guess...accused of being a vigilante and trigger-happy. I'll get through it."

"I'm sure you will. I am I am." He smiled at her. "Have you taken a Ritalin today?"

"I did just a little bit ago...gaw...you and Grace sure are big on me taken my meds."

Rocky laughed. "You bounce off the walls sometimes, sweetie."

"Rikki, are you ready? Do you need to prepare? We have thirty minutes." Grace interrupted. Her anxiety was much worse than Rikki's.

"I think I'm ready. How do you prepare for something like this? I'm just gonna speak from the heart. Try not to get angry and handle myself in a professional manner."

"Okay, why don't you focus on that until its time?" Grace didn't fancy Rocky there distracting her. She wanted all the bad publicity to go away and this was a chance for that to happen. Rikki didn't appear to be taking it seriously.

"Grace, stop worrying. Everything will be fine. I do have a concern about the hit man showing up. But if he does I'll deal with it as it comes. That's all I can do."

There's the Rikki I need right now. "I'm just making sure you know what you're doing. We don't need another disaster on our hands."

Rikki hauled Grace off to the side. "Having Rocky here is *not* gonna cause a disaster. I am focused. I'm calmer than you're used to. Like I told you, Rocky calms me...I don't know why. I know what needs to be done and I'm going to do it. Do ya feel me?"

"I feel ya. Never seen you like this. It's kinda freakin' me out." Grace admitted.

"Where will I be standing?" Rikki asked.

"I figure we'll do it outside. I think it will be a good turnout, so I have you on the steps and everyone can stand below you so they can all get a good shot." Grace had it all figured out.

"A good shot. The bad guys will have a good shot too." Rikki said.

"I meant angle...camera angle. Why did you have to say that?" Grace was a ball of nerves. "Let's pray."

"That's a good idea."

They joined hands and Grace prayed for protection and safety. They both felt better.

The media began to arrive and Grace instructed them where to set-up. At two o'clock Rikki and Rocky walked out. Rikki stood in front of the microphones while Grace and Rocky stood to the right side of her. Rikki was poised and calm. She was focused on what needed to be said. Grace and Rocky were anxious for her. They knew she would do just fine but as they looked out into the faces of the thirty some odd media people, they were both glad it was Rikki and not them that had to speak. The cameras all aimed at her, and all eyes focused on her.

"I'd like to thank everyone for coming." She began, making eye contact with as many as she could. "First, I want you all to know, I don't regret my actions in either of the shootings. With that said, I want you to also know that I'm not trigger-happy or a vigilante. I hate the actions I was forced to take. Nonetheless, given each circumstance I would do the same thing again. Greg Hayes had a gun to Grace's head." She pointed at Grace. "He wanted to see me suffer. He wanted to see me die. There was no question about that. I did what I had to do to survive; anyone would've made the same choice in that situation. I deal with unstable people everyday and in fifteen years I have never had to take such action. Tad Brackin came at me with a knife with every intention of killing me. He was disillusioned, disoriented and about to die. He was doing what he thought he had to do to survive – again, I did what I had to do to survive. I wish things could have ended differently but it was out of my control. To the viewers, I'm not out of control and I'm not a danger to society. For whatever reasons, I was attacked twice and I survived twice. I'm a firm believer that everything happens for a reason. I'm also a firm believer in God. I would protect a total stranger in the same way. That's just how I roll...its how I was trained. The reports you have been hearing from our fine media," she smiled, "are more for ratings than the actual truth. So don't believe anything you hear and only half of what you see. Dig deeper for the truth. Lastly, I'd like to thank Teryn Tennin for reporting the facts and not getting caught up in the hype of all that's happened in the last few days. I truly do appreciate it. Are there any questions?" Rikki smiled again anticipating the questions that would be thrown at her.

"Rikki, what did you mean by Tad Brackin was about to die?" Teryn asked.

"You didn't know? Tad had been stabbed twice. He was acting on pure adrenaline. What I call the adrenaline dump. Your body will dump adrenaline through your veins in times of shock, desperation or fear. Like someone drowning will often try to drown the person that came to their rescue out of fear. Another example, when you get scared, you shake or jerk or scream, sometimes even hit. You have no control over it. It's your body reacting to the adrenaline dump. In very serious situations, like Mr. Brackin was experiencing, all he knew to do was survive by killing whoever crossed his path. Unfortunately, it was me that crossed his path."

"How do you sleep at night?" Someone from the back row yelled.

"I'm human. I close my eyes and see Mr. Brackin charging at me with a bloody knife. Or I see Mr. Hayes falling to the ground. It takes me awhile to go to sleep but that's normal in this type of situation. I pray that in time it gets easier. How do you sleep at night slandering someone's name like you have mine? Is that okay? Wouldn't you assume that I have enough to deal with without adding slander?" Rikki tossed the question right back to the unknown reporter. There was no answer from the journalist.

There it is again. The evil lurking about. The precise sensation Rikki had at the hotel. *He's here. I feel him.* Rikki looked around scrutinizing everyone, everything around her. *Where is he? Who is he?* She ignored the questions being yelled at her. Finally, she looked to her right at Rocky and Grace. Both knew something was wrong.

"Excuse me. I have one more thing to address." Rikki's behavior changed to cold and callous, eyes narrowed and voice deepened. "I know you're here. You can bet your life...I will not sleep until you are *dead* or in custody. You will not get away with murder, not as long as I'm alive. I promise you this...I will find you. You will make a mistake. I'm in your head now and you second-guess everything you do. The end for you is very near...*very near.*" Rikki focused on a white SUV parked across the parking lot. She wasn't sure why. "Take a moment and get right with God because *I* will get *you*. I can feel your evil from here, and I'm not scared...not even a little bit. You're a coward in every sense of the word." Her black eyes darted around the parking lot, daring him to show his face. She knew he wouldn't—cowards never do.

"Okay, that's it. No more questions." Rocky grabbed Rikki by the arm. She had just threatened the murderer and he was furious with her.

"Who are you talking too?" Teryn Tennin yelled.

"Where is he?" Another reporter yelled.

The cameras were scanning the parking lot. They all wanted a glimpse of what Rikki saw. They didn't need to know there was nothing to see, that she purely acted on a gut thing.

Rocky and Grace pulled Rikki inside the office and locked the doors. "What was that? You did beautifully, absolutely perfect the way you handled the whole Tad thing. Then that? What the hell? It's a wonder you didn't get shot!" Rocky clenched his teeth and shook his head. He was visibly upset with her.

"He's here, Rocky. I felt him, just like I felt him at the hotel. It's the most evil sensation. I had to say something. He thinks he's so good, so sly. He's not. I will catch him."

"Rikki, you won over the media, I know the viewers were cheering you on. Then you go off sounding all crazy. Oh no, that didn't just happen. Wonder if I can talk them out of airing the last part of that." Grace was thinking damage control as she paced.

"That's probably the only part they will air." Rocky added.

"You guys...I don't care. I have to catch this guy. He's trying to kill Jade...she's next...I had to let him know he was stupid if he tried."

"You might be next now." Rocky growled. He pulled Rikki close and held her. "You never cease to amaze me. You worry me."

"It's okay...me and Grace prayed. We are protected. Have a little faith."

"She's right, we did pray." Grace agreed halfhearted.

"I still worry."

"Well, don't baby. This is how we roll."

"It is...its how we roll. She does something stupid and I pray." Grace managed a giggle. "I'm glad you have him. I think he will be good for you."

"Not as glad as I am! Hey, where's Lexi? I haven't seen her at all today."

"I told her not to come in." Grace said.

"She'll be mad she missed the good stuff." Rikki said.

"No honey...you're the only one that thinks what just happened is good stuff. I've never met her but I'm sure she won't be mad for missing that." Rocky corrected her and kissed her affectionately on the lips. "The swelling has gone down. I'm glad."

"Me too!"

18

ROCKY DROVE RIKKI AND Grace (against her will) to the morgue. They arrived early. Grace sat in the truck and waited while Rikki and Rocky went inside.

"Hello, doll." Melody greeted them in her white lab coat and big black hair.

"*O-si-yo* (hello), this is Rocky." Rikki said.

"Nice to meet you. Oh, Rikki, you really pulled a good one, impersonating me. Your friends were not happy. That Gates guy was furious. They waited for forty-five minutes. He mentioned something about suing you. I told him *I* wouldn't be filing a formal complaint."

"You failed to tell me about that." Rocky looked down at Rikki, curious.

"We'll talk later." Rikki giggled. "Sorry I put you in that situation, it was a last second decision I made. Maybe not the best one, but you were sleeping so sound. Does your neck hurt?"

"Gotta crick in my neck, that's for sure." Melody rubbed her neck.

"Jade will be here in a second to identify Tad."

"I've got him all ready. I don't think I've ever seen you so often during one investigation. You are filling my morgue."

"I'm not proud of that."

"I wouldn't think so." Melody shook her head then looked at Rocky. "So Rocky, how do you handle her?" Melody said flatly.

"With both hands firmly...I do, I do." He was cocky.

Melody laughed. Rikki didn't, she looked up at Rocky and gave him a dirty look but couldn't hide her smirk.

"Whatever." She finally said rolling her eyes.

Rocky cracked himself up. "It's okay, baby, I'm not complaining."

"I like the way you handle me with both hands." Rikki decided to take it one step further.

"Do you?" Rocky gave her an intrigued look.

"I don't want to hear anymore!" Melody put her hands over her ears.

The front door opened and Jade and Johnny entered the morgue. Jade was somber, still in her rocker outfit. Johnny looked worn-out. Melody wasted no time. She motioned them over to a drawer and pulled it open. Jade took one look at Tad and began to cry. Johnny didn't know what to do he felt awkward. He finally put his arm around her shoulder for comfort and she broke down and sobbed. Melody wasted no time pushing the drawer back in.

"That's my husband."

"I'm really sorry, Jade." Rikki was apologetic for shooting Tad.

"Is Miles here?" She asked.

"Yes." Melody answered puzzled.

"Can I see him?"

"Sure." Melody looked at Rikki with a question.

Rikki mouthed, "Her lover."

Melody pulled out Miles Casteel still looking at Rikki. Jade's sobs turned into an uncontrollable wail.

Rikki cupped her forehead for a second. "Jade, there's some paperwork."

"Okay." Is all she could utter.

After all the formalities Rikki, Rocky, Johnny and Jade stood in the parking lot. Rocky had walked over to his truck and opened Rikki's door for her as she spoke with Johnny and Jade.

"Do you know where you are gonna stay?" Rikki asked Johnny.

"We are real tired of hotels. She's okay with going to my house for a day or so."

"Okay."

Grace sat in the back seat of Rocky's truck. "See that SUV over there?" She asked Rocky.

"Yeah."

"It pulled up a few minutes after Johnny and Jade but nobody got out."

"That's weird."

The SUV spun out and raced through the parking lot aimed at Rikki, Johnny and Jade. Rocky took off running toward them.

"Rikki!" He yelled. Rocky shoved her out of the way of the speeding SUV. Rikki toppled over Jade as the SUV slammed into Rocky with a gruesome echoing impact. Rocky was airborne for thirty feet. Rikki jumped up and ran toward Rocky. Johnny pulled his weapon and began firing at the SUV.

Rocky ricocheted on the cement tumbling a few more feet. He lay in the parking lot lifeless. Rikki reached him within seconds. "Rocky! No!" She screamed. She knelt beside him. "Baby, talk to me!" She clutched his face in her hands. His blood oozed swiftly through his shirt. "Talk to me, Rocky! Hang on, just hang on." She kissed his lips. "You're gonna be okay, can you hear me?" She turned her head away from him, "call nine-one-one!" Her voice cracked as she yelled for help.

Rocky barely opened his eyes. Rikki was relieved. "There you are. Stay with me, help is on the way." She watched his blood soak his shirt. "Oh God please, please help him."

Rocky gazed at Rikki blankly his voice was barely a whisper. "I love you to death."

"I love you to death. Please hang on!" She looked around for anything to apply pressure to the blood flow. "You saved my life. I'm not gonna let you go!" She turned her head again, "someone bring me something!" She knew she needed something but wasn't sure what it was.

Rocky's eyes closed. "No! You open your eyes Rocky Payne! I love you so much! Don't you give up!" She kissed his face. She could see him fighting; his eyes opened again only this time they had a lethargic glaze.

"I love you to death." He repeated without moving his lips.

"Rocky, don't you do it! Don't you die!" Rikki cried. She had her hands over the wounds on his abdomen struggling to stop the blood flow. His blood seeped through her fingers, as tears streamed down her face. "Please, no, please, no," she sobbed. Her hands weren't enough to even slow the bleeding. Desperate, she flung her body across his abdomen. "Wake up...you hear me! Please wake up!" Rikki yelled, unintentionally saturating herself in Rocky's blood.

"Rikki?" Melody had hurried out to the parking lot when she heard the commotion. "Doll? He's gone." She said as gently as she could.

"No he's not!" Rikki moved up by his head and checked his breathing. Nothing. She began CPR breaths. "Come on, get a breath baby." She gave more mouth to mouth.

"Rikki...he's gone." Melody repeated.

"No! He is not gone!" She provided another breath.

Grace stood over Rikki horrified and weeping. "Let her try!" She screamed at Melody.

Rikki checked his pulse then crawled up on top of him and began compressions—then more mouth to mouth. "Rocky you aren't gonna die." She said while she administered more compressions. "This can't be happening." This was the most unbearable thing that could possibly happen. She continued CPR for what seemed like an hour. It didn't matter, she would've continued for days if there were a hope he would come back. She never lost momentum back and forth between compressions and breaths. Oblivious to everyone's pleads for her to stop, for her to let Rocky go. She had smeared blood from head to toe on herself and Rocky's body. Rikki acted on raw emotion, not something she had ever done before. She was disoriented and in distress.

"Come on Rikki, he's gone." Melody tenderly repeated. She had already told the paramedics Rocky was gone. There was nothing they could do. Melody recognized death when she saw it, after twenty-three years experience.

Grace had to do something. It was obvious Rocky wasn't going to live through this tragedy. *I have to steer her away from Rocky's body.* "I got the tag number and already called it in to Stone. He should have some news for us shortly."

Rikki finally stopped CPR and sat by his lifeless body. She ran her fingers through his hair not saying a word. Her heart was shattered into a million pieces. She struggled to breath, to swallow. Her throat felt like it had swollen shut. Grace sat down beside her. Their world had really spun out of control now.

"I should've included Rocky in our prayer. I didn't want him here. I thought he was distracting you. Then he saves your life." Grace had her own guilt.

"No, it's my entire fault." Rikki cradled his head in her arms and put her cheek against his. "It's all my fault." Her head was spinning accompanied by irrational thoughts. She felt Rocky's face beginning to get cold. "He needs me to spoon him." She whispered then uncrossed her legs and tried to lie next to Rocky.

"Come on Rikki. They need to take him now." Grace was bound and determined not to let Rikki spoon Rocky's dead body in the parking lot. "We need to let him go."

"He needs me to spoon him!" Rikki screeched. The sound of her own voice echoed in her head, like a slap in the face. *I've lost it. This is too hard. Just a few hours ago he surrounded me with his warm body…he made-love to me.* Tears streamed uncontrollably, "I can't do it. I just can't do it." She held tightly to his body. "I'm so sorry." Rikki fought for the strength, the courage, to walk away from the only man she had loved in fifteen years.

"You have to, Rikki. They're waiting on you to take him." Grace pleaded.

Rikki stood covered in blood with her hand over her mouth, in shock, as she looked down at Rocky's lifeless body. She couldn't wrap her brain around the image before her. Stunned she fetched a sheet from Melody. Before she lovingly covered Rocky's body, she slid his horseshoe ring off his right ring finger and held it tight. "*Wa-do* (thank you), Rocky. I love you to death. I swear I will not rest until I kill the man Who did this to you—to us." She whispered, and then walked away from him—forever. Her heart was so heavy and shattered that she wanted it to explode...for relief. A part of her died right then and there and was carried off with Rocky's body.

19

RIKKI SAT IN THE driver's seat of Rocky's truck, in a fog. Her feet didn't come close to the pedals, and she didn't want to budge the seat even an inch. She wanted it right where Rocky left it. If she didn't have to shift gears she would have managed to drive without moving the seat. As it were, she had to move it forward about a foot. As she drove to the office she swallowed the smell of Rocky that lingered in his truck.

Grace sat silently in the passenger's seat. Words would be inadequate right now. *I don't think Rikki even knows I'm here. She really shouldn't be driving. I don't think my best friend will ever be the same. Hopefully time does heal all wounds.* Grace watched Rikki and she felt her pain.

They parked in the back of the office and Grace got out of the truck and went inside. Rikki pulled her knees up to her chin and sat sideways on the seat. She honestly didn't know what to do next, she felt so lost and alone—numb. About the only thing she did know was she liked being in his truck.

Grace leisurely strolled out the back door and was surprised. Rikki was still there sitting in Rocky's truck. She opened the door, "Rikki? You alright?"

Rikki didn't answer.

"Are you going home?" Grace's concern skyrocketed. She immediately called Cricket.

It didn't' take long for Cricket to get to the office. She had been at Rikki's house with Gunner and Mallie. One look at Rikki and Cricket bawled. The dried and some still damp blood was startling. But more so was Rikki's incoherent demeanor. Cricket didn't say anything she went straight to her cousin and wrapped her arms around Rikki.

After a few minutes Cricket spoke, "come on I'll take you home."

"No. I'll drive Rocky's truck home." Rikki was stern.

"You okay to drive?"

"I'm fine." Rikki whirled around in the seat and started the engine.

"See you at the house." Cricket shut the door. "I'll take it from here." She told Grace.

Gunner and Mallie freaked out when they laid eyes on their mom. She didn't say anything to them—she couldn't. Cricket handled the kids while Rikki went upstairs to her room. The vision of their mom had them both in tears. They saw the pain in her eyes as she walked by—not the usual spunky, free spirit they were used to all their lives.

The mirror in her bathroom reflected a pitiful site. Rikki didn't care. She robotically removed her clothes, folded them neatly and placed them on a shelf in the closet. She had no intention of ever washing the clothing stained with *his* blood.

Rikki stood under the shower as Rocky's blood slid down her body and accumulated on the tile. She watched it whirl around the drain and disappear. She leaned against the tile wall and cried while the water splattered around her. *I don't want to rinse him away! I'm whining...I wanna to hear him say American or Cheddar.* His blood was all she had left to hold on too, now even it was gone. All she wanted to do was get in bed and cover her head. To function in day-to-day life would be overwhelming. Not doable. No purpose.

Rikki lay on her bed and stared at the wall. Gunner, Mallie and Cricket sat on the bed beside her. She had been lying in the same position staring at the same wall for six hours. Little did anyone know the amount of anger building within the depths of her soul. Anger at herself, anger at God, anger at the hit man, anger in a broad-spectrum. She couldn't forgive herself. She wished Rocky had let the SUV hit her. *I don't deserve this. All these years alone and I finally find someone. God, I know I'm not perfect but I don't deserve this. Is it my purpose to be alone and anyone I love is going to die? Is that the big plan for my life? I put my life on the line everyday to help other people and I can't have love? It's cruel.* She lashed out at God. *That's fine. I don't care. I'll find this guy who killed Rocky and I will kill him with my bare hands. Why not? I've killed before and I'm gonna do it again.* That was her last thought before her eyes slammed shut and she sank into a deep sleep.

"I thought she'd never go to sleep or move or anything ever again." Mallie whispered.

"I wish I knew what to do for her. I liked Rocky. He used to come over. I thought he was a good guy." Gunner added softly.

"I liked him too." Mallie agreed.

"I wish I knew what to do for her too. Sleep is the best thing for her right now. Let's go downstairs and I'll fix something to eat." Cricket told the kids.

"Chicken Ole sounds good and mom loves it." Mallie suggested.

"You're gonna cook at midnight?" Gunner asked.

"I don't know what else to do. So I'll make the chicken ole. Your mom does love it. She says it taps her taste buds." Cricket went to the kitchen and pilfered around for all the ingredients. A wave of sadness hit her. She sat at the table in the breakfast nook and cried. "How could this happen?" She whispered to herself. She heard one of the kids coming and jumped up and wiped her tears. She buried her head in a cabinet looking for a pan, actually hiding her tear-filled eyes from the kids.

"Do you need any help?" Mallie asked.

"Sure, you can open all the cans." Cricket sucked up the sadness and painted on a smile.

Upstairs Rikki slept, until her phone rang. "Rikki? We got a hit on the tag. We know who the guy is. Wanna meet me at the office?" Grace was wound up.

"I was having that dream about my mom again. It actually gave me a little peace."

"Sorry I woke you but I thought you'd want to know."

"I'll be there in ten minutes. I'm gonna sneak out so nobody tries to stop me." Rikki was already out of bed and putting on her shoes. "Grace? I'm going to kill him...you are aware of that, right?"

"Rikki you can't just kill him. Make him attack you or something first." Grace didn't try to talk her out of it.

"Well, yeah." She was already going out the french doors in her room and down the balcony stairs.

Guilt of leaving the house without telling Cricket and her kids got the better of her. Cricket didn't like receiving text message but Rikki sent her one anyway.

I got a lead on the hit man. Don't let the kids go upstairs...I left. Don't worry I'll call ya soon.

She felt a little better.

"Give me the scoop on this guy." Rikki said to Grace the second she opened the door. Grace thought she looked like the wrath of hell, but kept it to herself.

"His name is Vann Badger, from New York. Bad dude, a record a mile long. I'm waiting to see what comes back on his credit cards. I found his cell phone number too. I'm waiting for those records."

"You've been busy! Thank you Grace. I totally checked out of life there for a while. I even yelled at God." Rikki confessed.

"Can't say that I blame you. Your eyes are swollen. I can't remember ever seeing you cry. Maybe tear up but never cry. That was hard to watch."

"I do, did, love him."

"I know."

The credit card information printed out on the printer. "Here we go." Grace handed Rikki a few pages and she kept a few. They studied every inch of the new information.

Seven minutes flew by before either spoke. "Here we go. He's at the Downtown Hotel. We gotta find him before TPD does! I want this Vann son of a bitch!" Rikki was out the door with Grace on her heels.

They wasted no time getting to the hotel. He was on the fifth floor, room five zero eight. Rikki and Grace slowly approached the door. It was open. Officer Luke Hixon was cuffing Vann Badger.

Rikki barged in, pissed and uninhibited by the room full of police officers. Grace folded her arms and leaned against the wall and watched. Rikki charged at Vann, ramming the palm of her hand to his nose. Officer Luke Hixon stepped back. He didn't stop her, the rage she carried was apparent and frankly he didn't blame her. Rikki could do what he wanted too.

She had Vann Badger by the hair growling through her teeth. "You will pay for what you've done...here on earth and in hell." She slammed his head on the wall. He fell to the floor. No one knows how many times she kicked him until she pulled her gun. She saw Rocky's smile, his green eyes that calmed her each time she looked into them. She saw Rocky lying on the cold cement of the parking lot dead. *I wanna pull the trigger so bad.* Her breathing increased and her jaw line tensed. Her trigger finger tightened against the trigger. She fought the urge to pull it. *I'll get him another way.* Her trigger finger slightly relaxed. *I will make him pay for Rocky. It would be so easy though...pull it...kill him.* Her finger tightened all the way around the trigger, squeezing, almost to the seven pounds of pressure it took to fire. *I'm just gonna do it!* She took a deep breath and began releasing it slowly. *Take him out...*

"Rikki, don't!" Officer Hixon finally intervened. "You can't shoot him." The other two officers pulled their guns and aimed at Rikki. "Put your weapons away!"

Rikki was too far-gone…she couldn't stop the gun from firing. Suddenly she slung her arms downward and to the left, the gun fired in mid swing. Everyone's ears rung from the shot and the air smelled of gunpowder. The bullet lodged in the mattress. Rikki holstered her gun, her breathing quickened. She glanced toward Grace who hid her face in her hands. The hotel room was still—no one moved.

After a few awkward minutes Officer Hixon spoke up. "Rikki, get the hell out of here! I should confiscate your weapon! Can't believe you nearly shot him…"

Rikki bent down and got face to face with Vann. "It's *not* your lucky day…this is not over. You will think of me everyday while you're in prison. I'll make sure of it. My face will be the last one you see when you are put to death. And you will get the death penalty I'll make sure of that too."   She stood up and spoke to Officer Hixon. "Could you make sure he is put in the cell with that Raymond character I arrested a few months ago? I'll go have a talk with him later." Rikki pulled out her cell phone and dialed Johnny. "Let's go Grace."

"Johnny, bring Jade to my office in the morning around nine." She hung up.

"Way to make him attack you before you laid a hand on him." Grace said. "You didn't even question Vann Badger!" Grace was confused by Rikki's action.

"No. He didn't act alone. I could look in his eyes and see he's not smart enough to do anything without being told. I guarantee he's the stupid son of a buck that does someone else's dirty work. Besides with all those police officers there he wouldn't talk." Rikki's mind was reeling a hundred miles an hour. "At least he's in custody. Jade's not in danger of him anymore. It's the one pulling the strings that I want. You think Lyric hired a private investigator to hire a hit man? Then the private investigator could say he was hired to protect Jade?" Rikki thought for a minute. "That's possible but I'm not certain. Something else is bothering me and for the life of me I can't figure it out."

"Anything is possible." Grace agreed. "Like you could've gone to jail just now...that's possible. You possibly almost shot another man just now..."

"Shut-up!" Rikki's head was spinning.

In the hotel lobby Rikki sat down in a leather chair. She struggled to get her thoughts together.

20

THE LOBBY WAS QUIET at three o'clock in the morning. An image of Rocky at the hotel danced in Rikki's head. *He looked so small.* She placed the tips of her fingers on her temples. She wanted to remember every little detail about him. *When will this aching in my heart stop?*

"What's wrong?" Graced asked.

"Rocky." She paused and looked up. "He looked so tiny in here."

"He is not tiny." Grace smiled.

"Was...was not tiny." Rikki whispered and turned her head away from Grace. Her vision was blurred slightly from tears forming but she could still see Lyric trudging toward the elevators. "I'll be back." Rikki defied gravity all the way across the lobby. Her feet levitated through the air until she reached an unsuspecting Lyric.

Lyric's frail arm was in Rikki's grip. Lyric thought her life was over. "Get your key card and open this door." Rikki powerfully demanded.

Lyric did as she was told. "I know who you are."

"Good. Then you know what I'm capable of and right now I *want* to kill someone." She could smell alcohol on Lyric's breath.

"You aren't Melody. I've seen you on T.V. You are a beautiful woman."

"Oh please, save it. I could care less what you think about me." The door opened into the indoor pool area. "Hey! Get out of here!" She yelled to a late night swimmer.

"Excuse me!" He yelled back.

Rikki still towed Lyric by the arm. She moved promptly to the other end of the pool to be near the swimmer. "I said get your ass out of the pool and disappear." She let the butt of her pistol show.

"Are you crazy?" He asked.

"That's what they say." Rikki's eyes were narrow and black, locked in on the swimmer.

"You're...I...I know who you are." He bolted out of the pool, bypassed his towel and made a mad dash for the door.

"If you say a word...I will hunt you down." Rikki yelled after him. So much for upholding a positive public view, she didn't merely seem to be out of control—she was out of control.

She shoved Lyric into a poolside chair with little regard to her frail frame. "You're scaring me." Lyric dared to say.

"I don't give a flyin' flip lady. Because of you five people have died including someone very close to me. It's personal, so start talking. It would thrill me to death to leave you at the bottom of this pool."

"Not because of me!" Lyric declared.

"You better convenience me of that real fast. Why did you hire Abner Stickels?"

"To protect Jade."

"Right. Is that the story you came up with or is it the truth?"

"The truth. I knew Vann Badger was going to try to kill her."

"How did you know?" Rikki was impatient.

"I overheard him having a conversation with someone. I don't know who he was talking to but they said it was time for my husband and Jade to die."

"Your story makes no sense...lots of holes."

"What do you mean?" Lyric fidgeted in the chair.

"Well, for instance, how did you know Vann's voice? Do you know him personally...ever talk to him before? He doesn't seem like someone you would hang out with. I think you do know who he was talking too. And your body language...screams liar at me."

"I did *not* want anything to happen to my husband or my sister. I knew they were having an affair but I still didn't want them dead! It's my fault they ever had an affair anyway."

"I don't care about who had sex with who!" Rikki pulled her gun out. "You are gonna tell me who had Miles killed...right now." Rikki's conduct scared Lyric more than the gun.

Lyric began to cry. "I can't tell you. He will kill me too. I tried to protect them." She began to sob uncontrollably.

Rikki holstered her gun and rubbed her face with both hands. *It was right in front of my face the whole time. Dammit!* "If you want to live, go back to your room and pretend we never had this conversation. If you talk, so help me God, I'll shake you out like a rag doll and torture..." She didn't even need to finish the sentence. Lyric heard her loud and clear.

Rikki dug in her pocket and produced a button that matched the buttons on Lyrics jacket. She tossed it at Lyric. "And you were in your husband's hotel room to warn him?"

Lyric studied the button then her jacket. "Yes. He wouldn't listen to me."

21

IT WAS TOUGH FOR Rikki to focus on the facts of the case, but she tried to study every detail. It was not a good time to be alone at the office. The death of Rocky had her fighting tooth and nail not to slip into a fetal position and suck her thumb. Anger and revenge reared their ugly heads and she couldn't fight it any longer. It festered into a raging fit.

This is a nightmare...it's not real. Can't be real. Her heart pulverized in her chest. She panted for air. "Oh God! It is real!" The masked anger released as every item on her desk crashed to the floor. Undoubtedly, the flat screen monitor would never function again. She didn't care. The credenza behind her desk encountered the same treatment. Books, pictures, gun cleaning supplies, files and handcuffs plunged to the floor. "Now, I am an out of control vigilante! I know what I have to do." She placed Rocky's horseshoe ring on her thumb and spun it around, it was even too big for her thumb. "Today this will all be over."

Lexi appeared in Rikki's doorway, eyes full-sized as silver dollars, as she absorbed the mess in Rikki's office, including Rikki. "Good morning?" It was more a question than a greeting.

"Hello, Lexi. I'm so glad you still show up for work. I promise you this case is ending today and things will get better around here." Rikki acted like she didn't just destroy her office.

"I'll take your word for it." Lexi disappeared to her desk and immediately called Grace.

"Johnny and Jade should be here any minute." Rikki yelled to Lexi. She placed Rocky's ring in her pocket.

"Okay." Lexi was relieved. She didn't want to be alone with Rikki at this point in time. On the phone, she filled Grace in on the office condition and begged her to get there right away.

Johnny and Jade arrived right on time. Rikki was antsy to say the least. She was ready to put an end to this case and avenge Rocky's killer.

"Damn! What happened in here?" Johnny asked.

"I had a little accident. It's all good. Nothing that can't be replaced." Rikki was acting calm and collected, but distant and shrewd.

"You alright? You seem a little…I don't know…weird, even for you." Johnny was alarmed. The usual sparkle in her eye was gone, replaced by a distant, dead and hollow look.

"I'm great. Never been better." She didn't even look at him.

Grace stormed into the office in dismay. "Rikki, what the hell?" She assessed the damage in the office.

"A bomb went off…totally out of my control." She didn't look at Grace either.

"More like you went off." Grace didn't know what to do for her.

"I feel so bad. This is all my fault." Jade announced.

"Let's giddy up…I'm ready to end this mess." Rikki ignored Jade. She pulled her pistol out and pulled the slide back. A bullet ejected from the chamber. She dropped the clip and checked how many rounds she had left. The middle drawer of her desk slid open and Rikki grabbed a hollow point bullet from the box. She pushed the bullet into the clip and stared at it. *Fully loaded, that's what I like to see.* She rammed the clip back into the pistol and replaced a bullet in the chamber.

"Will you tell us where we're going?" Grace asked.

"Oh sure, Gates is hosting a gathering at the hotel. The mastermind will be there and I am going to kill him." She replied as if inviting them to a tea party.

Grace released a sigh. "Rikki, you can't walk up and kill someone...we've had this conversation before." She started to try to talk her out of it—again.

"Why?"

"You will go to jail. Who will raise your kids?" Grace tried to heave her back into realism.

"I won't go to jail. He's gonna try to kill me first."

"And what if he does?" Sadness overcame Grace as she watched her best friend sinking into a dark pit of loneliness and anger. *Lord, please help her.*

"It will be fine, Grace." Rikki said. "I know you just prayed."

*****

"Jade, ask Gates to read the will." Rikki instructed before she knocked on the door.

"He's expecting us right?" Grace asked.

"He should be." Rikki pounded on the door.

"I mean, we have an appointment, don't we?" Grace pried.

"Not exactly." Rikki confessed.

"Jade? What a surprise." Gates said when he answered the door.

"Good morning, Gates. We are here to read the will." Jade blurted.

"What? I'm not reading the will now. I have a flight to catch." He blocked the door.

Rikki shoved him out of the way and walked in. "You're not going anywhere until you read the fucking will!" She yelled on the verge of truly loosing control.

"Rikki!" Grace was astounded by her outburst.

Gates stuck his chest out. "Who do you think you are? Barging in here ordering me around. I am not reading the will." He was angry. "I don't even have a copy with me."

Jade followed Johnny and Grace through the entryway of the suite toward the sitting area. Jade wasn't prepared to find her sister, Lyric, seated at the dining room table saturated in fear. The estranged sisters engaged in a stare down. Neither knew what to say or do. A tear dropped down Lyric's cheek as she began to shake. Jade turned her head away when she felt the wetness of her own tears slide down her face. How did their lives get so screwed up?

"We are not leaving here until there is a reading of the will." Rikki said with her teeth clamped together, bullheaded. Her disposition was rigid to say the least.

Johnny, unsure about what was taking place followed Rikki's lead and positioned himself in the entryway, on guard. Gates would have to go through him to escape and that wasn't about to happen.

The way Rikki watched Gates with a glaze of rage in her eyes made him squirm. She wasn't there to intimidate him. She wanted him dead or alive. *How much does she know? How can I talk myself out of this? I'm not sure I can. I will not go to prison. Give her what she wants and maybe they will leave and I can disappear.* Gates had to think of something quick.

"I do know that Miles left most everything to his wife, Lyric. The specifics of his will escape me right now." He tried to be sincere and confident.

"That's what I thought you'd say." Rikki released her gun. "The truth is...he left everything to Jade...everything."

Lyric gasped. "What?"

"He made a new will in June...you get nothing." Rikki was relentless.

Grace's heart flopped in her chest. It was all coming together for her. *Oh dear God, please don't let her shoot them! Give her the strength to do what's right.*

"I didn't know." Lyric softly said. "That's the reason you planned all this?" She asked Gates but didn't need the answer. "He has blackmailed me for millions. We had an affair three years ago and I didn't want Miles to ever find out. It would have killed him to know his best friend and his wife betrayed him like that. Just like it killed me to know my own sister and husband betrayed me." Lyric sobbed. "You wanted me to inherit his millions so you could get your hands on it."

"I've always loved you, Lyric. Miles didn't deserve you. When he came to me and changed his will, I thought I could make it go away by having him killed and destroying the new will. And we could be happy again." Gates broke down. "I never meant for so many people to die." He moved toward the kitchen and leaned against the counter.

Rikki watched his every move. "That's like me hiring someone to kill Grace." She shook her head. "Why did Tad have to die?" She wanted answers.

"I didn't even know Tad was here." Gates answered.

"I called him after I hired a Private Investigator to protect Jade. I told him Miles was murdered and I was afraid for Jade's life. He came to help Jade." Lyric confessed through her tears. "I love my sister and I didn't want anything to happen to her."

Jade was speechless. The sight of her sister shaking and crying crushed her heart. *She tried to protect me.* Jade went to Lyric and got on her knees in front of her chair. "I love you too, Lyric." She cried. "I had no idea what you were going through. I thought you were behind all this." The estranged sisters hugged one another and sobbed.

Gates made a sudden move in the kitchen. Rikki aimed her gun at him. "Get on the ground...now!" She yelled.

Gates opened a drawer and grabbed a Beretta .40 caliber semi-automatic. Rikki took aim at his heart with her finger wrapped around the trigger applying steady pressure. A tiny squeeze would put a bullet through Gates' heart. *This is going to feel good.* Johnny had is gun aimed at Gates' head.

In one swift motion, Gates placed the revolver under his chin and pulled the trigger. His body slumped to the floor with a thud.

Jade and Lyric gasped and held their breath, each afraid to move.

Grace covered her face in shock. "I can't believe he just did that!"

"I can." Rikki was disappointed she didn't get to shoot him. "May you burn in hell, coward."

22

RIKKI AND GRACE WATCHED the officers bring Raymond through the door to the meeting room at the jail. Rikki had arrested him six months earlier. Not a nice man, just what Rikki needed at the moment. He sat down at the table not at all happy to see Rikki and Grace.

"Grace, know what I'm thinkin' right now?"

"As a matter of fact, I do...a brain floating in a jar."

"That's right. I don't know why the name Raymond makes me think of that."

"What do you want?" Raymond said, pokerfaced.

"I wanna make you a deal. Your new roomy Vann Badger... make his life hell...make him wish he were in hell. Kick his ass everyday...make sure he is raped everyday. I don't care what terrible things you can come up with...just do it." Rikki was callous.

"What's in it for me?"

"Well, it will give you something to do. And when you get out I will help you get right. Straighten your life out, so you never have to come back here."

"What did this guy do to you?"

"He has killed probably more people than we know, one of them Rocky Payne, someone very close to me. I could've killed him, but that would be too easy on him. Will you do it?"

"Like you said it will give me something to do. No mercy?"

"No mercy." Rikki said as she tapped on the door for the guard to open it.

"Do you feel even a little bad for doing that?" Grace asked. They walked through the jail and stopped at the security door. Rikki grabbed the bars and rattled it. Her way of telling the jailers to buzz them through.

"Not right now. I might in a few days. They'll move him to another cell when it gets real bad. I know I shouldn't feel so vengeful but I do."

"And getting revenge...does it make you feel better? Does it bring Rocky back?" Grace was going to make her point no matter what.

"Makes me feel better right now...don't bring Rocky back."

*****

Rikki was taken aback by the condition of her office, she had forgotten about trashing it earlier. "Wow, I had a *nu-da* (insane) moment, huh?" She picked up a few items off the floor and sat them on her desk.

"Something like that." Grace agreed.

Johnny had dropped Jade and Lyric at Rikki's office and went on his way. The bad guys were caught and Jade was safe, Johnny's work was complete. Rikki and Grace joined them in the lobby.

"I am so glad you two are getting a second chance at being sisters." Grace said.

"We are too. Thank you so much for everything. I never imagined things would turn out the way they did when I first came to you. I am so sorry for all you have endured in the process. I am a better person for knowing you both." Jade's sincerity was touching even to Rikki.

"Thank you, Jade." Grace said.

Rikki sat silent. *I need to tell Raymond to forget it. My tsu-sa-si* (revenge) *should be that the bad guys are caught and let the Lord handle it from here.* She wrestled with shame. *I'll go see*

him tomorrow. One day of hell for Vann Badger won't be that bad.
Maybe two days.

"Rikki, I want to give you something for saving my life." Jade carried an oversized leather bag over to her and sat it in her lap.

Rikki unzipped it and peered inside. She found four tickets to Bora Bora and stacks of one hundred-dollar bills. Rikki glanced up at Jade.

"Bora Bora is my favorite place to get away. You could use a little time off. Everything is taken care of. You will want for nothing and be waited on for all your desires." Jade explained.

"Thank you, Jade." Rikki half smiled.

"And that's a half million dollars...I know you can't put a price on Rocky's life...that's not what I'm trying to do. I just wanted to give you a bonus for your hard work and suffering." Jade seemed almost embarrassed.

"You're right...that doesn't begin to replace my Rocky. But thank you, Jade, you are very generous." Rikki was amazed by the gesture.

Wish Rocky was here to go to Bora Bora with me. She heard the last words he ever said to her, *"I love you to death."*

Gv-ge-yu-hi (I love you). Rikki was lost in thought.

Grace watched Jade and Lyric get into the Mercedes to travel back home to New York. She smiled—*good for them...they got each other back.* Their reunion touched her, made her want to call her own sisters.

"Earth to Rikki!" Grace yelled when she walked back in the office.

Rikki looked up, "I'm right here!"

"She could've at least given you a full million...after all this! She's got ba-jjj-illions and can only part with a half million, please! You saved her life and figured out who killed her lover... you were injured in a fight...you were blown through the air... and worse than that you lost Rocky! I would've been impressed with a million dollar bonus but this half million crap just pisses me off!" Grace blurted.

Rikki smirked, "I shot her husband."

"And for that she should've gave you two million! I think you did her a favor. Did you notice she wasn't even that upset about it?"

"Let's go to Bora Bora and forget about it!" Rikki paused. "There's just one thing I want to do before we leave."

"And what would that be?"

"I want to go to Rocky's house and ride Goose." Rikki smiled.

"You can't ride a goose!" Grace was mystified by the visual of Rikki mounting a goose.

"Goose is Rocky's horse, goofy. I want to ride him and smell him."

"You've always loved that horse smell. I like to sniff the saddles myself. Is this something you want to do alone or do you want me to come with?"

"I'll go alone. I figure riding Goose will be a good time for me to go to my safe place...behind a brick wall with my heart protected by a block of ice. And utter my farewell to Rocky. "

"I really wish you wouldn't do that. That's not how you need to heal from this."

"It's all I know. Alone...is all I know." Rikki shrugged.

*****

Goose perked up when Rikki entered his stall. The sight of him put an instant smile on her face and a smidgen of joy in her heart. She closed her eyes as soon as her arms were wrapped around his neck and inhaled deep.

"Hello Goose." She gently stroked him between the eyes followed by a kiss on the nose.

Goose kept an eye on Rikki as she yanked on the saddle. It was heavy but she was determined to carry it over to Goose and heave it up on his back. Goose was unusually patient. Of course, he was always more patient with Rikki than with Rocky. He would give Rocky fits sometimes—throwing his head and stomping around Rocky—that amused Rikki. Rocky didn't baby Goose like Rikki did. Goose knew the difference.

"Alright boy, are you ready?" Rikki said as she threw her leg over and perched up in the saddle. Goose was ready.

They moseyed down the trail through the woods. *The last time I was on this trail I was riding behind Rocky on a four-wheeler in the dark.* She sighed at the memory. Rocky drove like a maniac forcing Rikki to scream and hang on tight. He laughed at her, not paying attention to her pleas to slow down. Rikki realized she was smiling at the memory and was glad she had it. *He was as ornery as I am.*

The wind picked up and Rikki closed her eyes and tilted her head up to let it blow her hair back. Behind her eyelids was the clearest image of Rocky, with his green eyes fixed on her as he smiled. She never wanted to lose that image. Maybe if she squeezed her eyes tighter she could feel him touch her one more time. She tried so hard but the touch never came. She never wanted to open her eyes again. Tears welled up then streamed down her face. To get a breath was near impossible. Her lips parted to suck up some air with fast shallow pants that made her dizzy. The dizzy spell made Rocky's image begin fade. *No, no, please come back!*

Goose abruptly halted forcing Rikki to open her eyes. He had stopped at the edge of the pond. "Need a drink big boy?" She let him have his head. He bent forward to the water and snorted sending ripples through the pond. "I'll take that as a no." She raised her shoulder to her cheek and swept away her tears with a heart so heavy she could feel it laying in her chest beating with a vengeance. She pulled Goose's head up and steered him away from the pond with a swift kick. "Yaaaaww!"

Goose took off at a dead run. Rikki concentrated on the ride, the sound of his hoofs pounding on the ground, the squeak of the saddle and Goose's steady breathing. *Lord, please carry me through this time, I can't walk alone right now. I've never felt so helpless.* Rikki's spirit had finally been broken and crumbled. Goose never faltered—his stride long-drawn-out and rapid. He took Rikki on the ride of her life. They ran the distance end to end of Rocky's ranch. Rikki tried to ride the pain away. The longer she rode and prayed the better she began to feel. She had been feeling like a stranger in her own skin. To get away and back to basics is exactly what she needed.

The wind rushed across Rikki's face and through her hair as her body moved in sequence with Goose. *I have another guardian angel watching over me and his name is Rocky.* A full-fledged smile swept across her face. In an instant her heart didn't feel so heavy in her chest. *You will always be with me.* She pulled back on the reins forcing Goose to stop. Instinctively she reached down and patted Goose's neck then pulled his mane through her hand. He had started to sweat so they drifted back toward the barn at a normal pace. Rikki lost herself in the surreal nature around her and a peaceful sensation overwhelmed her. *Thanks Rocky.*

It was much easier to unsaddle Goose than it was to saddle him up. His ears slid out of the bridle and Rikki hung it on the wall.

"Thanks for the ride Goose." She wrapped her arms around his neck again and took a deep breath. "You smell good."

She combed his mane with her fingers then ran her hands down his neck and across his belly. "I'll check on you ever so often." She draped her arms over his back and leaned against him. The expectation that Rocky would dart through the barn door at any moment made her hang on Goose longer than she intended. Her eyes scanned the barn absorbing everything that reminded her of Rocky. At last she slid her arms off Goose's back. He turned his head to see her with one eye, she patted his jaw. "I'm gonna be okay, right boy?"